plagued

KNIGHT PACK BOOK 3

Elissa Daye

This is a work of fiction. Names, characters, places, and incidents are products of the author's imagination or are used fictitiously and are not to be construed as real. Any resemblance to actual events, locations, organizations, or persons, living or dead, is entirely coincidental.

World Castle Publishing, LLC
Pensacola, Florida
Copyright © Elissa Daye 2019
Paperback ISBN: 9781950890958
eBook ISBN: 9781950890965
First Edition World Castle Publishing, LLC, December 30, 2019
http://www.worldcastlepublishing.com

Licensing Notes
Cover: Melissa Davis
Editor: Maxine Bringenberg

CHAPTER 1

The old woman held her hand like a vise. Kendall never expected the fortune teller to get this involved in her readings. "I see a dark cloud over your shoulders."

Kendall fought the urge to snort. Dark cloud her ass — it was an endless void if you asked her. She could pinpoint it to an exact moment in time really, but she'd rather not voice it. It made her sound petty and ungrateful. Kendall was neither of those things — she was just tired of living in someone else's shadow. No matter what she did, it was never good enough. Closing her eyes, she chastised herself for her uncharitable thoughts. Thinking ill of the dead was something else she could add to her list of faults, apparently.

"Your life is about to change."

That was true. Her life was about to change, not that Kendall had a choice in the matter. The twenty-four-year-old had been called home to take care of her mother, but things were not looking good at all. Elizabeth Pearson was in her final stage of life. The cancer had spread throughout her body like a wildfire, a harbinger of death and destruction. The only thing Kendall could do was help keep her comfortable when she visited her in hospice. Kendall had done what she could to make the small room feel more like home. She had tried to get her mother to come home with her, but her mother didn't want to be a burden to her.

When Kendall wasn't at the hospital, she was at home going through all the things that would need to be sold or donated. Her mother had already done a fair amount of paring down. At least the basement and attic had been cleared out. Now all that was left was her mother's room and the one room no one dared touch. It might sound silly, but even now, Kendall was afraid to touch an inch of Hannah's room. It had become a memorial to the child they had lost way too young. Kendall had not stepped into it for quite some time. She didn't want to admit how much she missed her sister. That felt too much like a weakness.

"Your mother walks in this world and the next." The woman jerked her hand away and smoothed some of her dark hair behind her ears. "But you know all this."

"Yes."

Of course, she knew that. She lived it every second of the day. The only reason she was here today was to find out what would happen next. Kendall was like a boat without a sail. She had no direction, no way to figure out what she wanted to do next. Her life had not always had a path, just a journey that never seemed to get her to where she wanted to be from one moment to the next. She was fluid like that.

"You're not here for that. You're here for him, yes?" Esme smiled at her. "He is a handsome man, the one who haunts your dreams."

Kendall sighed. That he was. All she knew was his name. Kameron Knight. Kendall had every detail of his face memorized from the one photo her sister had sent home from Afghanistan. The two of them had been thick as thieves there, from what Kendall understood. Of course, she had been about fourteen herself when Hannah had first entered the service. He had been the man she fantasized about for so long. Was it unusual to have a crush on her sister's last love? She looked down at the table and tried to push out those thoughts. It wasn't like she was going to run into him any time soon.

"You yearn for one, but run from another."

That was also true. Kendall had been running for quite some time. Her ex-boyfriend always seemed to find her. Thankfully, playing nursemaid to her mother had kept her off his radar. Perhaps the binding spell she had cast a year ago had finally worked. Alistair had his own philosophy when it came to magic. He believed that magic was his to manipulate, that the power was his to control. Alistair had never learned the rule of three, that everything he put out in the world could come right back to him threefold in the long run. His magic was only part of the problem, though. That man was wicked through and through. She shivered just thinking about the man she had barely escaped.

The rule of three had affected her in ways she could not even understand. Her jealousy of her older sister had exploded out of proportion. She blamed herself for her death, for all the hateful thoughts she had just before she left for her last deployment. Hannah's courage, her service to their country, had outshined Kendall's attempts to gain any kind of attention from her parents. They always told her to be more like her sister, but Kendall was too much of a screw up for that. Study harder, make the honor roll, get into a good college. To this day, Kendall could feel the censor from her mother. Hannah would have been much better at taking care of her mother than she was. Kendall sucked at it. That was probably the real reason her mother wanted to be in hospice at the hospital.

"When your mother passes from this world, you must move quickly."

"He's coming for me again, isn't he?"

The blonde shivered in fear. She didn't want to think about the man who had taken her innocence and left her with emptiness and fear. Kendall had been seventeen when Alistair had entered her life. He was twenty-two, and everything a troubled teen wanted in a boyfriend. The more she upset her parents, the better Kendall had started to feel. The wholesome teen who had devoted her life to dance had turned into a gothic ball of hate under his tutelage. By the time she tried to break free from him, she had lost every bit of herself. Manipulation and control were second nature to him, as was the cruelty he treated her with. Kendall had come to believe that was all she deserved. That was what the others had thought too. Even now, the rhetoric flooded her consciousness.

"Yes." Esme looked away from her and shivered. "He's become stronger."

Kendall closed her eyes and tried not to think of the overbearing tyrant who had taken her innocence in ways no girl should ever experience.

Esme touched her hand. "It will take great courage, Kendall, but you will find the light at the end of this dark tunnel."

"I don't deserve it."

Her eyes met Esme's, and she shut her emotions down before the fortune teller could try to comfort her. There was no hope for her anymore. Kendall already knew that. What little happiness she had in this world had been stripped away from her long ago, the minute she had lost the only thing that made sense to her.

"You will need protection when your mother passes. I know a place where you can start a new life, child."

"What's the point, Esme? He will just find me. He might even kill me this time." Kendall just might let him.

She had died long ago, the moment the soldiers had knocked on their door. Kendall had been the one to answer the door. The image replayed in her mind over and over. Her perfect sister was no longer coming home. Her parents would never see their favorite child again. Instead, they were stuck with her. Kendall often thought her father had deliberately drunk himself into his death just so he could be back with Hannah. It wasn't like Kendall had needed him at all. Anger often implied strength, and while she had held plenty of anger inside her, Kendall's weakness had been invisible to the rest of the world. To everyone except Alistair. He had a knack for finding the weak holes that let him get his talons into his prey.

"He will try, that you can be sure of. Your life has a purpose you haven't even realized yet, my dear. Don't give up on it."

"It gave up on me a long time ago, Esme." Kendall pulled her hand away and pulled money out of her pocket. "Thank you for your time."

"No, child. I will not take your money." Esme held her hands up.

7

"I earned it honestly."

Kendall felt her feather's ruffling. She may have done some horrible things in her past, but she was on the straight and narrow now. When she wasn't taking care of her mother, she was working her ass off cleaning houses for a small cleaning company.

"That is beside the point." Esme pulled out a piece of paper and wrote down a name and address. "When you are ready, contact Marina. She will help guide you to the next stage of your life. Help protect you."

"I can take care of myself."

Nonetheless, Kendall took the paper and slid it into her pocket. She wasn't sure what she was going to do for the next stage of her life. It was probably a good thing she had learned to take care of herself when she was younger. When her mother passed, there would only be her. Kendall tried not to think of it too much, but the end was inevitable. Her mother slept more and more each day. The doctors told her it could be any day now.

"Just because you can doesn't mean you should. You've been alone for far too long. So has he."

Kendall looked across the table at Esme. She pulled the picture out of her purse. "He needs her. Not me."

The image of her sister with the mysterious man stared back at them. It was plain to see they cared for each other. This was the kind of love she had been looking for all her life. Someone to hold her up when her world fell down around her, a pair of strong arms that weren't afraid to see the flaws beneath the surface. Someone to love her unconditionally when she couldn't conjure any love for herself. No one had done that for her. She had always had to carry her own weight and had long ago gotten used to disappointing the ones she loved. Life was one big pile of shit. She didn't see that changing anytime soon.

"We don't get to decide what other people need, only what we are capable of giving."

Kendall gestured to herself. "There's not much here, Esme. I'm a walking train wreck."

"Ah, but you are still walking," the woman teased her.

"Barely. Just barely."

Tears filled her eyes, and she squeezed her eyelids shut to ward them off. She had learned that crying got her nowhere long ago. It was a weakness she could not afford.

"This, too, shall pass."

Why did people always say that? It wasn't like she had gallstones, or had swallowed something that would expel itself from her system. It would only be more of the same, only this time she'd have to find new people to disappoint.

"Thank you for your time, Esme."

"You'll be back, Kendall," the woman predicted.

Kendall picked up the picture from the table and shoved it into her purse. She smiled at Esme. "Is there ever a chance I'll find some kind of happiness?"

"It's waiting right out there for you, Kendall. You have just to reach for it." Esme had a knowing smile on her face.

"Nothing's ever that easy."

"And yet it is. If you'll excuse me, I need to refresh for my next client."

"Right. Sorry. Thank you again." Kendall allowed Esme to pat her on the hand.

"All will be well, child. All will be well."

CHAPTER 2

As she walked out of the tiny shop, she barely looked where she was walking and ran smack dab into a strong muscled body.

"Oh, I'm so sorry. Excuse me."

"Any time," a warm voice chuckled.

Kendall looked up at the face in front of her and almost died of mortification, especially when he looked at her as if he recognized her. Kendall stepped back and shuffled slightly under his perusal. All these years of fantasizing about the man before her, and here he was in all his buffed glory. His face was covered in a thin beard that she was half tempted to run her fingers across. His green eyes seemed to compliment his reddish-brown hair. His voice was like silk.

"Kendall Pearson?" He asked her softly.

"Ye...yes?"

Kendall swallowed loudly and grimaced as she heard the slight gulping sound. He was even more magnificent in person. Kendall looked back at the shop and wondered just how Esme had known what was coming next. And how in the world did he know her name?

"You look just like your sister." Kam looked as if he had

seen a ghost.

"My sister?" She feigned curiosity, even though she knew damn well that's who it was. Boy, would he be surprised when he found out she was nothing like her sister.

"Hannah?"

"Yes. Hannah was...."

She looked down at the ground. How could she describe her sister? Brilliant, compassionate, brave, beautiful? How about perfect; that covered it all, right?

"I'm Kam Knight. We served together before.... Well...." The light in his eyes faded slightly, and he cleared his throat. "Do you have plans right now?"

"Excuse me?"

Was her voice too high? It sounded a little edgy. She felt like a school girl talking to the quarterback. *Get a grip, Kendall.* He was probably just being nice, after all. It wasn't like he was actually interested in her, just in the memory her sister had left behind.

"Have you had lunch yet?" He smiled softly at her.

"No...I mean, I haven't eaten yet."

Not that she would be able to eat a thing with him anywhere near her. The picture really had not done him justice; that, or the years had only enhanced his attributes. If only time were as kind to everyone else.

"There's a cafe right around the corner. I was just heading there. Care to join me?"

Join him? Her mind was definitely not in the right place, but how could she pass up the chance? "I'd like that."

Kam looked at the door she had come out of. "You a friend of Esme?"

11

"Uhm...well, a new one, I suppose." Kendall didn't really want to get involved in that topic, especially since the woman had spoken about him. She was curious as to how he knew her. "Do you know Esme?"

"One of my mother's friends."

His smile could have lit up a cloudy day. It was clear that Kendall was in way over her head, and all he was doing was being nice to her. She really needed to get a grip, or she was really going to make a fool out of herself.

"Really?"

Kendall didn't know what else to say. Was his mother a witch too? Hannah had never mentioned that. Then again, Hannah had been a straight-laced Christian girl, not a pagan like her. Kendall had always been attracted to the paranormal, even as a child, but had not realized at the time that she was a witch. It certainly wasn't something she advertised to the world around her, especially after Alistair had used her beliefs against her in ways she would never completely recover from.

"Yes. They go way back."

The two of them walked in what was probably just a normal silence to him, but one that filled her with an unease that made her almost sick to her stomach. She knew she was going to make a complete ass of herself. Any fool could predict that. If she had just waited a few more minutes before she left the shop, this would never have happened. Then again, she wouldn't have seen him standing before her in flesh in blood instead of a faded slip of paper.

He gestured to the door in front of them. "Here we are. Allow me."

Kendall's hand brushed against his before she could

retract it. She wasn't used to anyone holding the door open for her. She almost stuttered over her words. "Oh, thank you."

Something flashed across his green eyes when he smiled at her. Kendall's breath caught in her throat as she was mesmerized by it. When she finally looked away, she imagined her face must be fifty shades of pink. By the time they found a table, she was feeling completely tongue-tied, and that was not like her at all. Kendall had always been far too outspoken for her own good. That had been a major contention between her and her parents. Sometimes she had wished she could change that. She had never meant to be so difficult. Kendall had just never fit her square peg into the round hole that everyone wanted her to.

"So...," Kendall said when there was an extended pause.

"So." His gaze was secretive, which made her feel slightly uneasy.

Kendall shuffled her feet under the table and tried to swallow the shyness that seemed to erupt around her. Before she could stop herself, her foot came out of her mouth, and she found herself returning to old habits — making a fool out of herself. "So, can I be honest with you, Kam?"

"Sure." Kam was now looking at her curiously.

"This is really embarrassing." *Shut your mouth right now, Kendall,* she begged herself, but once she started, she could not seem to stop.

"It can't be that bad," he teased her.

"No...it's pretty bad, actually." She reached inside her bag and pulled out the picture of Hannah and Kam and slid it across the table. "I wasn't entirely honest with you."

"How's that?"

"I knew who you were. I mean, I would have known you anywhere."

She closed her eyes and looked away from him, swallowing uncomfortably. What was wrong with her? That was a stupid thing to do. Was it wrong that she almost wished someone would come and rob the place right now just so she could have a distraction from herself? The nervousness, the feeling that for some reason, fate had put him right in her path, it all rotated inside her like a dangerous cyclone.

"She was a beautiful woman." Kam touched the picture softly, and his smile was filled with a sentiment that crushed all her teenage dreams right on the spot.

Kendall realized in that moment that Kam was still in love with her sister, which made this infinitely more embarrassing. Why in the world had she brought it up? Stupid, stupid, stupid. Time to put that foot back in her mouth before she put the final nail in her coffin.

"Yes. She was. Hannah used to talk about you all the time. She called you her rock."

Kendall saw the water the waitress set down on the table and was thankful for her arrival.

"What can I get you two?"

"I'll take today's special," Kam answered without taking his eyes off the photo.

Kendall almost wished she could have been anywhere but there at the moment. So much for fantasies. They never lasted anyway.

She looked up at the waitress. "Sounds good. I'll have the same." Turning back to Kam, she said, "You must miss her." Kendall found herself consoling the man who might have carried a torch for Hannah all those years. Her life had come full circle, as her inadequacies, her inability to be her sister, was finally cemented in stone.

"She was a good friend."

Friend? Who was he kidding? Anyone could tell they had been more than friends. "Friend? We had the impression.... Well...we thought the two of you were—"

"Together?" Kam looked at her thoughtfully.

"Well, yeah." Weren't they? They practically looked like they had just kissed in this photo, their faces were so close to each other.

"In another lifetime, perhaps."

"So, you weren't...."

"Lovers?"

Had they suddenly turned the temperature up in this room? Kendall took another drink of water. "Goodness. I'm sorry. That's rude of me, and completely none of my business."

"You can ask me anything, Kendall. To answer your question, no. We were not lovers."

"But, you would have been." Kendall pushed forward with her curiosity, another one of her faults.

Kam chuckled at her determination. "You're a heavy hitter, aren't you?"

"I'm not known for keeping my mouth shut when I should absolutely know better. You'd think I would have learned my lesson by now." She smiled apologetically. "I'm sorry."

"Don't be. You're refreshing." Kam put his hand over hers.

Kendall fought the urge to pull it away. Her skin tingled where his fingers touched hers, and it was unnerving the hell out of her. She shook her head at him. "I'm not, not really."

"And you're beautiful."

Kendall blinked. Was he really looking at her? Was she still at home dreaming? Had she stepped into some alternate dimension? "I...um...thank you, I guess."

"Can I ask you a question, Kendall?"

"Uh...sure." She had the urge to hide under the table, melt into the floor, or evaporate on the spot. Kendall was terrified of what his next question was going to be.

"Why do you carry this picture around?"

She nibbled her bottom lip, wondering what answer would be the best reply right now. Anything but.... "The truth?"

"The truth."

Kendall looked down at the picture, refusing to make eye contact. For some reason, she knew he would know if she was lying. "When I was younger, Hannah sent me this picture of the two of you. I...well...you see.... You're going to laugh."

"I doubt it." Kam's voice was soft as his thumb made soft strokes over her hand.

"I was a teenager and had this mad crush on a man I had never even met. I fantasized about him for years."

"And now?"

Her eyes flew up to his, and she saw what looked like desire brewing there, although it had been some time since anyone had looked at her like that. "I'm sorry, what was that?"

"You still have the picture with you. I just wondered if you still fantasize about me." He grinned at her.

Kendall removed her hand and reached for her glass of water. She closed her eyes as she drank half the glass. "I...I think I should go."

His eyes flashed golden as he put his hand firmly on hers. "Stay."

One word, and she felt herself cemented in place. Her throat swallowed, and she had the distinct impression that he was watching her every move. "I'm not my sister. I have a nasty habit of embarrassing myself and others. And a big mouth. I have a big mouth too. It tends to get me into a lot of trouble."

"I think it's delectable. And I like trouble."

Delectable? As in delicious? He couldn't mean that. And what kind of man admitted to liking trouble? Kendal sighed. "Now you're making fun of me."

"I would never." Kam held his hand up in front of him. "I promise."

"I've told you one of my secrets. Now you tell me one of yours." Kendall crossed her arms over her chest. She wanted to change the topic to anything else but how she may or may not feel for the handsome man before her.

Kam reached into his wallet and pulled out a photo, which he slid across the table. It was one of the last pictures she had taken with her sister. "I have a picture too."

Kendall touched the picture and smiled. "She was everything I could never be."

"She used to tell me about you. Hannah loved you very much."

Kendall rolled her eyes and shook her head. "She tolerated me, just like the rest of them. I'm not that palatable."

"Someone did a real number on you, didn't they?" Kam smiled softly at her.

"You must miss her." Kendall slid the photo across the table. He'd said they weren't a thing, but he carried her photo, so apparently, there was more to the story.

Kendall heard her cellphone ring and looked down into her purse. Her face must have gone white, for Kam's voice was filled with concern. "Is everything all right?"

"No...I have to go."

Kendall pushed away from the table and raced for the door. She made it outside before Kam caught up to her.

"Wait, Kendall."

She stopped in her tracks, and her hands made tight fists at her sides. Kendall should not have gone out today. Normally she was at her mother's side, but she had needed some fresh air. Dallying with him, she had missed her chance to say goodbye to the last person she had left in the world. She would never forgive herself for this.

"Please, Kendall. Wait."

"I waited too long, Kam." Her answer was a hollow whisper as tears slid down her face.

"What was the message?" Kam refused to budge.

"While I was indulging in a selfish fantasy, my mother died alone. I should have been there. She was all I had left, Kam."

"You're not as alone as you think," he whispered.

"Stop." She held up her hand. Tears were threatening to melt away the last bit of her strength.

Kam pulled her into his arms before she could refuse. She felt the strength in his comforting embrace as he held her tight. "Where is she, Kendall?"

"What? Why?"

"Because I'm going to take you there." He kissed the top of her head softly, or she imagined he did.

"You don't have to do that, Kam." She pulled away from his arms and felt the warmth fade around her. It was as if it had never been there at all. "I have to go."

"Wait, Kendall. You don't have to be alone."

"It's what I deserve."

She turned around and walked as fast as her legs would carry her. Kendall had parked her mother's car at the hospital, so she had a long way to go. How could she have left her? Her mother didn't have anyone else there with her. Kendall took only small comfort in the fact that her father and sister were waiting for her on the other side.

She heard footsteps behind her and found herself being trailed by him. Kendall turned around and faced him. "What are you doing?"

"Going with you."

Angry tears slid down her face. "Stop it, you can't do that."

"Why not?" He asked her softly.

"I don't...I can't...." Kendall sank onto the bench beside her as her grief took over.

Kam held her tightly against him, stroking her hair as he whispered softly. "You're not alone, Kendall. I'll take care of you."

She looked up at him with tears streaming down her face. "Why?"

"One day, I'll explain. For now, just let me be here for you." He brushed her tears away with his fingers and kissed her forehead, a gesture that was probably far more innocent than it felt.

Heaven help her, Kendall found something stirring deep inside her. She sighed as she leaned her head on his shoulder again. It was good to have someone to lean on, even if she didn't really have the right to do so. "Thank you," she sniffed slightly.

"Whatever you need, Kendall. I mean that."

She looked into his eyes and got lost inside them. It would mean so much more if he wasn't just doing this out of some obligation to her sister's memory. Not that she had any right to be jealous. She didn't really know the man. Kendall had no claim over him at all, but she was being pulled to him in a way she could not describe.

He looked as if he were about to kiss her, but he stopped just a few inches away and cursed softly. "This is not the time for that."

"I'm sorry?" Kendall blinked. Why did it sound like he was talking to someone else?

"Nothing. Let me drive you to the hospital."

"Thank you, Kam." She put her hand on his cheek. "It means more than you know."

Kendall had not wanted his help, but she also did not want to be alone. While she knew he would not be hers for too long, she would take whatever she could get. Besides, at the moment she really could use a friend. The next few days were going to be hard to deal with. While he might only be here for the moment, she'd take it.

CHAPTER 3

As she entered the room, she saw her mother lying peacefully in the bed. Kendall dried her eyes and tried to keep herself calm. She sat down in the chair next to her bed. "I'm sorry I missed you."

The nurse smiled softly at her. "This happens more than you think. Sometimes they wait for you to leave so they can spare you the pain."

Kam cleared his throat from the doorway. "I'm sure she wasn't alone."

"Right." Of course not. Even in death, Hannah was sure to be the perfect daughter, by her side then and for the rest of eternity. Unlike Kendall, who was always too preoccupied with herself to be there for her. She closed her eyes and tried to slow the thoughts that rotated in her head.

"I'll give you a few moments." The nurse nodded to her and left the room.

Kendall reached for her mother's hand and held it tightly in her own. Just hours before the skin had been warm to the touch—filled with fragile life, but life nonetheless. Now her mother was just an empty shell of the woman she had been before.

21

She felt Kam move behind her but didn't turn to look at him. "Do you think they really are together?"

"Yes, I do." His hands rested on her shoulders.

"Good. I would hate for her to be alone. It's a horrible feeling." Tears threatened to spill over her eyelashes, but she could not afford the luxury.

"It is." His own voice was filled with a sadness that was palpable.

"I wasn't an easy child."

"She loved you, Kendall," he assured her.

"Yes, I suppose she did, but I never made it easy for her." Kendall sighed and tried to keep those thoughts at bay. She would never make it through this if she thought about all the times she had let her family down. There were too many to list.

"Take it from me, mothers are made to be resilient. My mother raised five boys. We've put her through enough hell to topple the strongest woman, and yet she loves us regardless." His hands massaged the tight muscles in her shoulders.

She relaxed against him. His words had done what a lifetime of reassurances couldn't. "I loved them all, Kam. I just wish I had told them more when they were alive."

"They are always listening, Kendall."

Releasing her mother's hand, Kendall put her hand on his and leaned against his strength. "That's kind of you to say."

He cleared his throat. "Do you want a moment to yourself?"

"No. I'm done. She's not here anymore. There's a lot I need to do." Kendall pushed away from the bed and stood up.

"What can I do?" Kam's eyes were clouded with an emotion she did not understand.

"I...." Kendall didn't have the right to ask for anything, really. She didn't like the idea of going home to her mother's empty house again, but she had no choice, really. "I need to go home. There's a lot to be done."

"Let me take you there."

"I have to move my mom's car." A tear fell down her face, and she wiped it away angrily.

"Then let me follow you home, Kendall. I don't think you should be alone right now."

"That's kind of you, Kam, but—"

"It's not kind, Kendall. It's selfish." A slow grin slid across his face.

"How's that?" She narrowed her eyes on him.

"I want to know where you live."

Right. He probably wanted to see Hannah's room. Her mother had kept it pretty much the way it always had been. She was actually surprised he had never come to see her family before. "If you want to follow me, that's fine. There's very little food in the house right now."

Did she just imply she wanted him to stay for dinner? Was that presumptuous? Perhaps, but right now, she wasn't exactly in the right frame of mind.

"We can order something," he suggested. "Besides, you never ate your food."

"Right." That was a waste for sure. It couldn't be helped, though. "Just let me talk to the front desk to have the body released for the next step."

"Take your time. I'll wait here."

Kendall walked over to him and reached up to kiss him on the cheek. Kam turned his face at the last minute, and their lips touched. Kendall sucked in her breath and stepped away. Her hand flew to her lips in surprise. "I'm sorry, that was.... I—"

Kam put his hand on her face. "Look at me, Kendall."

Her eyes flew to his, and she felt small beneath his gaze. She did not understand the emotion that was etched inside them. Kendall's eyebrows narrowed in confusion. "I didn't mean to overstep. Call it a lapse of mental judgment."

"Pity." His lips turned up slightly at the corners.

She left him before she could confront him on his meaning. It was for the best at the moment. Kendall was filled with volatile emotions that could easily explode at any moment. One moment she wanted to push him away, and the next — well, she had improper intentions.

After filling out the paperwork for the proper handling of her mother's body, Kendall was pretty shaken up. She had spent months knowing this was going to happen, but the actual reality of it was more devastating than she imagined it would be. Her mother had taken care of her father's arrangements. Kendall had been in another state altogether at the time. She had only come home when her mother had gotten sick and needed care. At the time, she had been a little resentful, but the months had passed, and her feelings had changed. What she wouldn't give just to have a few more years with all of them in her life. Now it was far too late for that.

Kendall returned to the room and found Kam sitting in the chair next to the window. His face was relaxed, and his eyes were closed — he almost looked asleep. With the sun shining in from the window, he almost looked like he was glowing. Her heart seemed to beat faster in her chest as she memorized the details of his face. The chiseled chin with a slight dimple must have gotten him out of a fair amount of trouble as a child. Kendall could not help wondering what that gentle scruff of hair would feel like as it slid across her skin. She wanted to run her fingers across his lips to see if they were as velvety smooth as they looked.

Kendall gasped when his eyes opened with a fire brewing deep inside them. "I...we...."

"All sorted?" His face was now filled with a mixture of concern and something else she could not quite place.

"Yes. I'm ready to go home. I have all the contact numbers there."

When he stood up and walked closer to her, she was reminded of a panther stalking its prey. She blinked and shook off her thoughts. This was not the time or place for lustful thoughts. He was here for purely innocent reasons, and from a sense of duty to Hannah, she was sure.

"You really don't have to—"

"Kendall." His voice was almost sharp when he stopped before her. His finger stroked her chin as he tilted it to look into her eyes. His expression softened. "Stop pushing me away."

"I'm not trying to. It's just that you really don't owe us anything."

"I'm not here out of duty, Kendall."

"Then why are you here?" Kendall asked him curiously.

"That I will explain in due time. Let's get you home." He opened the door and gestured for her to move through it.

"Fine, but it's a little messy right now."

"You could be a hoarder, and I would still come," he replied.

"Okay."

She took a deep breath and looked back at her mother one last time. A lifetime of apologies surfaced inside her. If only she had been better. It might not have changed the outcome of her mother's death, but she wouldn't be left with the guilt that circled inside her. She had been the cause of a lot of stress for her parents. Sometimes she wondered if that stress had taken far too much of their lives.

"It's going to be all right, Kendall."

Kendall didn't answer him. She turned away and started down the hallway. Her defense mechanisms were starting to kick in. Every time she lost someone, a piece of her hardened and shut out the world around her. She heard Kam's footsteps next to her, but she did not allow herself to feel the warmth of his comfort, nor would she allow herself to become attached to his presence. He would leave as soon as his misplaced sense of duty left. She only hoped that it was sooner rather than later.

As she left the hospital, the air around her seemed even more volatile than usual. At first, she thought it was just her imagination. She scanned the parking lot, and as she did, she felt the hair standing up on the back of her neck. Something was very wrong. She turned to find Kam looking around them. Did he feel it too?

"I'm just up that row." Kendall pointed to the white Camry.

"I'll follow you."

Kendall nodded at him and turned away. She was starting to feel a little unnerved as she moved down the rows to where the car was parked. By the time she made it to her car, her heart was racing in her chest.

"So...you thought you could hide from me?" A cynical voice made her jump for more reasons than one.

"Alistair!" Kendall turned around to find him standing against the van next to her. Had she not been so distracted, Kendall would have sensed him earlier.

"Who's that man?"

"It's none of your business." Kendall's chin jutted out in anger, and she tried to keep herself from smashing her teeth together.

"Everything about you is my business, Kendall. Or had you forgotten?" His hand reached out and jerked her head back by the hair. "You're mine, Kendall."

"Let go of me right now." She sneered at him, and her anger crackled around her. Sparks were erupting from her hands as she prepared to take him down if she had to.

"Never." His mouth was so close to her that her flesh felt like it was about to crawl.

Kendall reached up and pulled her hair out of his hands. Her foot stomped on his, and her knee shot into his groin.

"Bitch!" he snarled at her. He reached back his hand to slap her, but it was caught midair.

A loud roar erupted from Kam as he jerked the man around and slammed his fist into his face. His eyes flashed with anger as he grabbed onto Alistair's shirt and lifted him a few inches from the ground. "Don't you ever touch her again."

"Who the fuck are you?" Alistair squirmed slightly as he tried to free himself from his grip.

"Your worst nightmare if you ever lay a hand on her again."

"Why the fuck do you care? She's barely worth the effort, man. A cold fish." Alistair wiped the blood away from his lip and spit on the ground at Kendall's feet.

Kam set him down and snarled at him. "You don't get to talk about her like that."

"What's it to you?" Alistair shrugged his shoulders. "Are you sleeping with him, Kendall? Does he get your rocks off better than I did? As I remember, you were quite willing—a little inexperienced at first. She does this thing with her tongue that—"

Kendall's face blanched. She felt herself shaking uncontrollably. "Leave me alone, Alistair!"

She didn't want to be reminded of all the things that man had made her do. Years of torture and pain climbed to the forefront of her mind, and she could not push them back. No one knew what he had done to her. She had hoped no one ever would.

"You heard the lady. Kick rocks." Kam's voice was shaking with fury.

Kendall didn't look up to see if Alistair had listened. She sat against the hood of the car and tried to control the shakiness that was racing through her right now. Trapped in memories that had been her own personal nightmares, Kendall found it hard to breathe. She was frozen in place, unable to calm herself down.

"Kendall…." Kam's voice was soft, almost a whisper.

Tears fell down her face. She didn't deserve his concern. Guilt and self-loathing had been her companions all throughout the years she had been with Alistair. He had wielded them as weapons and controlled her like his own personal slave for way too long.

"Look at me, Kendall."

"I can't." Kendall looked down at the ground and felt the tears stinging her face.

"Please...." His voice coaxed her.

She gave in, against her better judgment. What she saw in his eyes nearly took her breath away. Kindness, compassion. It tortured her more than she could voice. "Don't look at me like that."

"Like what?"

"Like you care." The sadness in her voice was only a small reflection of the sorrow she felt deep inside. This day was the absolute worst day in the history of all days ever.

"I *do* care." His hand stroked her face. "More than you know."

She jerked away from him. "So did he. Look where that got me."

Kendall stepped away from him and opened her door. Throwing her purse inside, she was about to sit down when Kam pulled her against him. His mouth was on hers before she could stop it. His fingers stroked the outside of her cheek as his lips moved gently against hers. She felt something soft and gentle unfurl inside her, like a flower starting to open its petals to the sunlight that streamed down on it. In a matter of seconds, he rewrote the vicious cycle inside her head and soothed the darkness away.

When he broke the kiss, Kendall was breathless. Her eyes shot up to his, not prepared for the raw desire that was painted inside. She was confused and enlightened at the same time. Her experience in men was extremely limited. Alistair had been the only one, and he was never gentle.

"I'm nothing like him, Kendall." His voice was raw with emotion.

"I have to get home, Kam." She didn't, not really. The things waiting for her could be done tomorrow, but she didn't want to stand here in this parking lot with him. Especially with her thoughts in such a confusing jumble.

"Let's go then." She held up her hand to object, but he cut her off before she could. "I'm not letting you out of my sight with that asshole around."

"Fine."

Kendall gave in without a fight, even though she knew better. She was three steps away from falling head over heels for the man she had always fantasized about. Kam was far more dangerous than Alistair because when he decided he was done toying with her, Kendall would be left with a heart so shattered she would never be able to piece it back together. And still, even knowing this, she was heading down the path to destruction.

CHAPTER 4

When she pulled into the driveway of the house, Kendall knew it was the first of many lasts for her. As the last living relative of the Pearson family, the house would be passed down to her, but it held too many memories from her childhood. She did not want the constant reminder that she had failed to be the daughter her parents had deserved. She only hoped that one day she would not feel like the colossal screw up that she had been most of her life.

She turned off the car and sat there quietly. She had been here without her mother for the past few months, but today was different. Kendall was afraid to walk inside. She almost jumped when the car door opened.

"Are you coming?" He smiled at her.

"Yeah, I just...."

"It gets better, Kendall."

"Best to rip off the Band-Aid?" She asked him softly.

"Sometimes." He offered his hand. "Besides, you're not alone."

Then why did she feel like the only person left in this universe? She wanted to ask him. She was still trying to figure out what he was doing there. And why had he kissed her?

Pity? That would be just her luck. A pity kiss from her sister's cast off. Kendall couldn't quite imagine why her sister would ever turn him away, though.

Kendall did the unexpected. She took his hand and stood up. "Thank you, Kam. I still don't know why you're here."

Kam looked thoughtful before he responded. "I have my motives, Kendall, but that can wait."

"Motives?" Her eyebrow rose curiously. "What kind of motives?"

He cleared his throat. "Can we go inside?"

"You're not going to take advantage of me in my weakened emotional state, are you?" She teased him.

"I'm trying not to," he admitted.

"Excuse me?" She saw his rueful smile and narrowed her eyes on him. "Maybe I should send you packing."

"Will you?" He stepped closer to her, and she fought the urge to run.

His mouth was so close to hers that she could stick her tongue out and lick it. She wondered what he would do if she did. Kendall felt her cheeks blush before she whispered, "No."

She moved away from him and opened the door to let them inside. Anything to put some space between them. The house was in different states of disarray, as Kendall had already been getting rid of some of her mother's things. There was so much to take care of that it started to feel overwhelming. She picked up the binder with the contact number to the funeral home as well as the attorney. Her mother had not told her what was entailed in the estates, only that the attorney would be able to assist her with it.

Kendall turned to see Kam watching her quietly. "I have phone calls to make. Make yourself at home."

"What can I help with?" He asked her.

"Food?"

"On it." He smiled at her and pulled out his phone.

Kendall walked into the small office and opened up the binder. She spent the next three hours calling anyone that needed to be informed. She had to make the final arrangements, but everything took time, and she just wanted it done. Her mother wanted to have a small service for people, nothing huge at all. Her body was to be cremated, and her ashes would be interred in the family plot.

Kam knocked on the door and interrupted her for the fifth time since she had started. She was about to make another phone call. "You need to eat, Kendall."

"I have to call more people." Kendall rubbed her temples as the stress took its toll on her body.

Kam walked over to her and put his hands on her shoulders. He kneaded the knots that were gathered around her neck. "You need to take a break, Kendall."

"I can't." It was true. She just wanted it all to be finished. Then she could work on figuring out the next step of her life.

"You have to let me take care of you."

"I can't," she answered him again.

"Why not?"

"Because you're just a mirage," she whispered. "You're here today, but you'll be gone tomorrow, and then I'll be back to where I was before."

"And where was that?"

"Dreaming about a man who doesn't exist." She sighed.

A tear slid down her face, and she wasn't sure why she was crying this time.

"Come here, Kendall." His voice was soft yet demanding.

Kendall stood up and felt his breath against her neck. She refused to turn around, for she didn't want to see the pity etched on his face. Pity was for the weak. Kendall refused to be weak ever again.

Kam slid his arms around her and pulled her close to his body. She felt the gentle comfort in his embrace, and her mind fought against it. Kendall tried to pull away, but he refused to budge. Turning around in his arms, she was ready to give him a piece of her mind, but the expression on his face took her breath away. He looked tortured.

"Do you want to see her room?" she asked him.

"Whose room?" He seemed a little confused by her question.

"Hannah's." She moved away as his hands dropped from her.

"Why would I want to see that?"

Kendall had already walked away from him, knowing deep inside he was there out of some misplaced duty for the one he still mourned. "It's down the hallway."

Kam followed after her without a word. It was enough of a confirmation to her. She opened the door and waited for him to step inside. When his feet didn't budge, she turned to look up at him. His expression was guarded.

"Don't you want to see her things?"

"No," he answered matter-of-factly.

"It's been untouched since...." She didn't finish that statement.

"Where's your room?"

"Right next to it. It's not as…what are you doing, Kam?" She felt herself being scooped up in his arms.

He didn't answer her at first. Instead, he kicked her door open and stepped over the threshold.

"Kam, why are you…?"

"Stop talking, Kendall."

He let her legs fall to the floor. Her body slid against the length of his, and she shuddered in reflex. His mouth was on hers before she could say another word.

His lips were hard and defined as they moved over hers. Kendall felt the heat that passed between them and fought the urge to wind her arms behind his neck. When his tongue pushed inside her mouth, she sighed against him. Her traitorous arms ignored her and pulled him closer to her. She should be pushing him away, but she just could not help herself. Real flesh and blood Kam was so much tastier than any dream she'd ever had.

When he broke the kiss, Kendall was having trouble thinking at all. All those times, she had fantasized about him in her room with her. She felt embarrassment fill her from head to toe.

Kendall saw the gold light flash in his eyes again. "Why do your eyes flash like that?"

"Sorry?" He asked in confusion.

"One minute they're green and the next they're like liquid gold."

He looked visibly shaken. Kam ran a hand through his hair as if he were trying to figure out the appropriate response. "There's a lot to tell you, Kendall. A lot that you're not ready for yet."

"I'm stronger than I look." Her chin jutted out as if to demonstrate. She put a hand on his chest and moved a little closer to him.

Kam closed his eyes. "I'm not."

"What could be so bad, Kam?" Her hand touched his face, and she saw a haunting pain on his face as he pulled away.

"We should eat, Kendall. I'll heat you up a plate."

"Chicken," she accused him. Kendall had no idea why she was pushing it, but she could not seem to let it go.

"Kendall," his voice warned her.

"What?" she asked innocently. It was as if she had done a complete tailspin. She waited for his explanation when moments ago she had been ready to push him away completely.

"I'll tell you over food, Kendall."

"Fine." She crossed her arms over her chest. "Don't think I'll forget."

Kam chuckled as he followed her out of the room. "I knew you'd say that. Let me heat you some food."

"I just have one more call to make."

"Kendall."

"Fine. But I have at least twenty more calls to make, and they are not going to make themselves."

"You can call people tomorrow, Kendall." His voice told her he was not going to let it go any time soon.

"Fine." She sighed and followed him out of her room. Kendall was still trying to figure it all out. What had brought on this need to take care of her? Didn't he have anything else he needed to do?

Kendall went into the living room and started to box up the things that were still sitting on the shelf. Her mother would probably want her to keep some of them, but Kendall had no need for them. She would keep the photo albums and some of the nostalgic things, but for the most part, she would be sending it to anywhere that could use it. If it were up to her, she would live in a one bedroom apartment somewhere with as few possessions as possible. That would probably be her next step, actually.

"What are you doing, Kendall?"

"Boxing stuff up. I need to get everything out, so we...." She paused and closed her eyes. "I can put the house on the market."

"You don't want the house?" he asked her softly.

"This place never felt much like home to me, Kam. It's just a reminder of never being good enough." She shook off her thoughts.

"I can help with that, Kendall. I have a family of strong and able-bodied brothers who can have this packed up in a matter of hours."

Kendall pursed her lips together. "I don't understand you, Kam."

He handed her the plate in his hand. "Eat."

"Okay, but only because you are supposed to tell me what's on your mind."

"Eat."

She took a bite of the pasta and chewed it slowly. After swallowing it, she set it down. "Talk."

"Eat more." He looked almost nervous.

"Fine, but you need to start talking." Kendall ate a few

more bites and waited to see if he would actually start to talk.

"I'm not like other men, Kendall."

"Okay...." She knew that already. Most men would have left her crying in a puddle.

"I...I don't want to scare you off."

She smiled softly at him. "Have you met Alistair?"

He flinched slightly. "That asshole...he's—"

"A mistake that keeps showing up no matter how much I try to get away from him. But this is about you right now. Not me. Just spit it out."

"I'm a werewolf."

"What?" She looked at him as if he'd lost his mind.

He cursed softly. "Damn it."

"Wait...hold on. Just give me a moment. You're an actual werewolf?" She looked down at the ground and tried to process his words. Kendall wondered if Hannah had ever known. "Did you tell Hannah?"

"No." That one word showed the strain he was under.

"I can't imagine she would have taken that well." Kendall grinned at him.

"And you?"

She nibbled on the bottom of her lip. "I've never met one before."

"Does it disturb you?"

Disturb her? Not really. She was more intrigued than anything else. Kendall had no idea what to tell him really, but it was clear that he was waiting for her answer.

"The truth?"

"Yes." His eyes were tormented as he waited for her answer.

"I find myself...." She looked down at the ground again. "Even more fascinated with you than I was before."

When she looked up at him, she saw the relief on his face. Kam had apparently been thinking the worst. "Fascinated?"

She blushed and looked away from him. "Is that pathetic?"

"It's flattering."

Flattering? Kendall sighed. "Was there anything else?"

Kam's phone dinged, and he pulled it out of his pocket. "Damn it, Killian."

"Everything all right?" Kendall asked.

"I have to go." Kam looked apologetic.

"Oh. Okay."

He stood up from the chair, his face now covered with an expression she could not read. "I'll be back, Kendall."

Right. It was totally normal to tell a girl you're a werewolf, and then leave as quickly as humanly or werewolfly possible. Kendall doubted he would be back. He probably had only told her to scare her off anyway. "Bye, Kam."

As if sensing the doubt running through her mind, Kam walked over to where she sat and knelt before her. "I *am* coming back, Kendall."

His finger stroked the outside of her cheek right before his mouth covered hers again. The soft heat of his mouth on hers made her wish he wasn't rushing off. There was something brewing between them that she didn't quite understand, but she wanted to know more. Kendall had never felt his way for any man before, and it scared the hell out of her. When he broke the kiss, Kendall shivered slightly.

She watched him stand up and walk away. As he made his way to the doorway, she called after him. "There is an extra key on the counter."

Kam stopped in his tracks and turned around to look at her. His eyes flashed bright, and she imagined that he was trying to get a hold of himself. "That could be trouble."

"Promise?"

He growled softly and clenched his fists at his sides and continued on his way. She could have sworn she heard him whisper, "I'm going to kill him."

Kendall did not have to follow him to know he took the keys. She heard the metal slide on the counter. Smiling to herself, she picked up the plate of food and sighed. She still wasn't convinced that Kam wasn't acting out of some kind of pity or misplaced duty to her or her sister. She'd try not to think about it for the rest of the day. Kendall still had a lot of work to do.

CHAPTER 5

Kam was ready to spit nails by the time he made it to where Killian was waiting for him with the others. "What is so bloody important?"

"What's got you so hot under the collar?" Killian asked him curiously.

"Nothing." Kam did not want to tell the others anything. He'd had far too much grief from them to last a lifetime already. Being the oldest, he should have found his mate a long time ago.

Karter sniffed the air slightly and smiled. "Who's the girl?"

Kam glared at him. "None of your business."

Kyle snorted. "Getting you laid is everyone's business."

Killian threw him a warning glance. "Don't listen to him, Kam. He's not getting much either."

"Hey, I get mine." Kyle grinned ruefully.

"Want me to smash his face for you?" offered Karter.

"Nah. Let him keep his pretty face for now. It's his only saving grace." Kam snorted derisively. "Why are we here?"

"Nasty mess out in Witch's Hollow tonight. Some dark casters have been brewing up trouble," Killian explained.

"What kind of trouble?" Kam hoped it wasn't like the last trouble that had come into Witch's Hollow. That demon had almost cost the life of Karter and his wife, Lila.

"We're not exactly sure yet." Karter looked exhausted.

"Kids keeping you up again?" Kam asked him.

"Teething babies are no joke. The boys are keeping us all awake. And Taela may look all sweet and innocent, but a cranky six-year-old is nothing to shake a stick at."

"How's Lila holding up?" Kam was almost jealous of their good fortune. What he wouldn't give to start a family of his own. He'd been waiting for his mate for a while now, knowing she would come when she was ready.

"She's exhausted. And extremely fertile," Karter sighed.

"Already?" Killian shook his head at his brother. "You gotta learn to keep it in your pants, brother."

"Hey, don't look at me. She's the one who instigated that mess." Karter smiled ruefully. "And I can't seem to refuse her."

"What are you going to do if it's more multiples?" Kyle teased him.

"Pray for sanity." He grinned at his brother. "Good thing I have enough land to add on to the house."

"Are we ready to head out yet?" Kam interrupted him gruffly.

He didn't mean to sound so angry, but his brother had touched a nerve inside him. Kam was happy for Karter. His brother deserved to be happy, they all did. Was it so wrong to wish for what he had? He thought about Kendall's soft lips against his and felt himself go hard. It had been far too long. He wanted her more than he could admit. His desire was a hunger inside him, one that he wanted to feed.

He wasn't the only one hungry for more. Kiego was hard to manage right now. His wolf had made his intentions known a long time ago. The minute Hannah had shown him a picture of Kendall, the wolf had howled inside him. At the time, he had felt guilty for his thoughts. She was barely old enough to desire, and yet the wolf knew even then that she was the only one he would accept. He wasn't proud of the lustful thoughts that had ripped through him at the time. Even less proud of breaking Hannah's heart. She had wanted more with him, but Kam held her at arm's length, breaking her heart.

That guilt had eaten at him. A slow depression had fallen over her, making her distracted when she was on duty. This distraction, he was fairly certain, had led to her death. Hannah had walked right into an ambush and was killed by the line of fire. He had wanted to pay his respects to her family, but even then, he had known that if he stepped anywhere near Kendall, he would not have been able to control himself.

What would Kendall do if she found out that he was responsible for Hannah's death? He was afraid she would push him away. If she did, he would be alone for the rest of his life. His wolf could only take one mate once he stopped prowling. Kiego had barely let him prowl at all, even in his younger years. When Hannah had shown him that picture, his entire world revolved around one girl who was far too young for him to mate with.

"We have to go to the table." Killian broke through his thoughts.

"The table?" Kam swore under his breath. "You know we're not supposed to cross those lines."

"I do, but we are also obligated to the lands there, Kam. We have to risk it." Killian's eyes were fierce and determined.

Kam nodded at him. He knew that the lands would always be part of their blood. Their family had been bound to this area since their father had claimed his mate, a witch from the camps near Witch's Hollow. While they protected all the people near the hollow, there were a few less deserving. The dark casters were always up to no good, but as his mother had always explained, light could not exist without the dark. The two complemented and contrasted in ways the universe had determined long ago. The same could be said with any magical entity. Where there were guardians like the Knight pack, there were also werewolves that destroyed any living thing in their paths. The Knights had made it their job to keep the other kind far away from their home turf.

"Let's go." Karter nodded to the rest of them. He was the first to shift into his wolf form.

Kam closed his eyes before letting Kiego take over him. His skin pulled into itself, and a loud howl erupted from his mouth as the pain of the shifting settled through him. The pain was worth the immortal strength his wolf gave him. While the Knights would not live forever, their lives would be extended as their bodies fought off the destruction that came with aging. Their healing factor had been greatly increased too, which often allowed them to heal their mates.

The four of them traveled as fast as their four legs would carry them. Only the slight pad of their paws and the whisper of fur could be heard in the darkness. The animals of the forest had gone deep into hiding. The silence had passed eerie several hours ago.

When they reached the outskirts of Witch's Hollow, the wolves paused. The hollow was protected by a magic older than time, fueled by the light workers and dark casters from the area. It was unclear as to where the dark casters resided. Kam assumed they lived in the dark recess of some moldy cave. The witches lived in their various small houses and huts in the camp that was only a few miles away from this very clearing. They liked to be close by to keep an eye on the balance of power that rushed through the ley lines. Ley lines were imbued with an energy that was ingrained deep in the earth, a combination of magic and electromagnetic energy that created the pulsing core of the ground beneath their feet.

Killian was the first to return to his human form. "That looks like a body."

Kam shifted and looked to where Killian pointed. In the middle of the table altar, a small, frail body was lying on top. "I need to get a closer look."

"I should go." Killian puffed out his chest.

"If it's a trap, I have far less to lose than you do." It was true. Killian and Karter had families they needed to think about.

"I've already entered once before," Killian interjected.

"That was to save your mate. I have no attachments; therefore, I'm the one who should go."

"What about me?" Kyle's chin jutted out defensively.

"You want to be the first to head into the hollow?" Kam challenged him. He saw Kyle falter for words. "I didn't think so."

Kam stepped into the clearing and tried to keep his breathing calm. If he allowed his fear to take over, the magic around him would sense it. Fear was one of the greatest manipulators.

When he finally crossed over the invisible lines that cycled the energy around him, he looked down at the witch on the table. She appeared to be younger, perhaps in her early twenties. Her body was completely malnourished, and she had marks on her wrists as if she'd been held captive. The pool of blood soaking the stone beneath her made him want to howl loudly in protest. This was a waste of human life. Whatever had killed her was not like the demons that had taken over the area before. These wounds were human made, from some kind of dagger or knife. Kam slid the hair from her face, and couldn't get over how much the woman resembled Kendall. The dark blonde hair was stained with dirt and grit, probably from wherever she had been held.

"She's gone," Kam shouted back to the others.

"We need to bring her to the camp so the witches can send her to her next life," Killian called to him.

"On it."

Kam gently retrieved the body from the stone and cradled her in his arms. They could have left her there and called in the officials, but the police department did not make it a habit to interfere in the hollow anymore. They were more superstitious than departments in other places, having seen their fair share of inexplicable deaths in the area. Kam thought that made them lazier than other departments, but his opinion would not get him far. It was also better to keep the Knight family off their radar. If there was knowledge of the wolf pack here, it would make it harder for their families to live and protect the lands around them.

Kam carried her to the edge of the clearing and set her down on the ground. "This was a man-made wound."

"Dark caster?" asked Kyle.

"Perhaps," answered Killian.

"They know better than this!" Kam clenched his fists at his sides. There was an understanding between the magical beings in the area. No sacrificial rituals, especially the kind that involved humans. Kam didn't like to see dead animals either, but that was a whole other can of worms.

"They do. We'll have to shake them down to find out the truth behind this." Killian nodded to Kam. "Let's carry her to the camp."

Kam nodded to his brother and picked up the woman's legs. The four of them would carry her to the camp. Kam sighed. This night was definitely not going as planned. First, Kendall lost her mother. Then he nearly let his wolf take her regardless of her grieving. And now this, escorting a dead body through the forest. He had promised to return to her house, but he had a feeling that would be a bad idea tonight. His thoughts were far too dark at the moment. Kendall did not need to be surrounded by them. She was probably better off without him anyway.

CHAPTER 6

After making the rest of her phone calls, Kendall spent the majority of the evening packing up as much as she could. When she ran out of boxes, she started to pull out trash bags to continue the process. She was bound and determined to get as much done as she could. Plus, it distracted her from the fact that Kam had walked out of the house over six hours ago. It was now almost midnight, and she was finally running out of steam. At least she had finished her mother's room.

Kendall looked at the empty space before her. While there was still furniture inside the room, every drawer was empty. She had only kept the jewelry in her mother's box. She would keep a few of the pieces and sell the rest. Kendall had no emotional attachment to them. At twenty-four, she was still young, but she was also pretty sure her life would not include any children to pass these things down to. It was less than likely that Kendall would ever find someone she trusted to let into her life like that. Plus, she had a feeling that the internal scarring inside her would prevent her from having them.

Kendall shuddered as she tried to push those thoughts from the forefront of her mind. It had been a while since she'd last thought about it. She blamed Alistair's appearance today. Kendall still could not figure out how he had found her. She had been extra careful to keep herself invisible to his magical reach. Had her weakened state made her shield waver slightly? She really needed to do something about that, but unfortunately, all the rest of this took precedence.

Stretching her arms over her head, a loud yawn left her body. Clearly, Kam wasn't coming back tonight. It was probably for the best anyway. She was a walking disaster that he didn't need to experience. He would always remain the man she fantasized about, but the dreams would be entirely more detailed now that she had actually met him in the flesh.

Kendall sighed and turned away from her mother's room. She walked to the bathroom across from her room and decided to wash the grime from the day off. Turning on the water, she waited for it to heat up. When the water was hot enough to scald her flesh, Kendall turned it down just a hair.

She stepped under the streaming drops and sighed. Hot showers were one of her favorite treats. It was the simple things that often carried her through her days, especially when she had to filter through the crap her life had handed her. It wasn't like she didn't take responsibility for her own actions. She did. It was just that there were quite a few shitty things that happened, with or without her assistance.

Squeezing her eyes shut, she tried to block out the nasty thoughts that circled inside her mind like a rabid animal ready to rip her apart without a moment's notice. Kendall put her head against the wall of the shower and took shallow breaths in and out. Before she knew it, she slid down to the bottom of the shower, shaking with the sadness that had threatened her sanity all day long. It would be far easier if she didn't have to outlive everyone else. Kendall sat there huddled in the stream of water. Her sorrow outlasted the hot water, and even when the water turned freezing cold, she was frozen in place, her tears cascading down her face. She never heard the door open.

The door to the shower opened, and Kam turned the water off. Kendall barely acknowledged his presence. He climbed into the shower and lifted her up in his arms. Cradling her against his body, he reached for the towel hanging near the shower and wrapped it around her. "I'm here, Kendall."

She rested her head against him, the tears no longer falling. A numbness had started to filter through her body as the shivering started. She shook against him as he carried her to her bed. All she wanted to do was fade into oblivion in the shortest path possible.

Kam sat on the bed with her nestled in his lap. His hands started to work the towel over her skin. "You're almost blue. Damn it, Kendall. Why didn't you get out of the water?"

She didn't even look at him. Her eyes barely blinked as the melancholy surrounded her. She was familiar with it. Alistair had been the first one to wield it as a weapon. Maybe he was doing so right now, or maybe it was just the grief working its way out of her system. Either way, the sentiment was familiar. Maybe not comforting, but something she knew like the back of her hand. She had been fighting it off for so long. Right now, she didn't have the strength.

Kendall was vaguely aware of the towel rubbing her skin gently. When it ran across her breasts, she felt a finger skim across it, and she sucked in her breath. Kendall blinked as a tremor worked its way through her. "Kam?"

"I'm here, Kendall."

She closed her eyes and tried to fight the emotions churning through her. When she opened them again, she looked up at him. "I don't want to be alone."

"You don't ever have to be alone again." He ran a finger across her face, and she let out an audible sigh just before his mouth came down to hers.

His hands continued to dry her off while he kissed her. When his tongue slid inside her mouth, she found his heat comforting. The dull pain that had filled her earlier had changed to something unfamiliar to her. It was as if she were waking up for the first time.

He broke the kiss and let his forehead rest on hers. "You're so beautiful, Kendall. Irresistible."

"And yet, you seem to be pulling away." Kendall sensed his restraint. She didn't want him to hold back out of some sense of duty or guilt. Every inch of her wanted to know what it would feel like to be his, if only for one moment in time. Kendall wrapped her arms around his neck and licked his bottom lip. She knew she was playing with fire, but she couldn't help herself.

Kam growled slightly as he took her tongue into his mouth. She felt his finger flick against one of her nipples, and she whimpered against him. Her stomach clenched as his tongue mastered hers so easily.

When he pulled away from her, his breathing was shallow. "I shouldn't be doing this, Kendall."

"Because of Hannah?" She asked him in a hollow whisper.

"What? Yes…no…maybe." Kam looked away from her.

"You should go, Kam." Kendall crossed her arms over

her chest and looked down at the floor. Her sister's memory would always be there to remind her of everything she couldn't be, everything she didn't deserve.

"I'm not leaving."

"Why not? Everyone else has." The bitterness in her voice wasn't lost on either of them.

"I'm still here." Kam caressed her cheek.

"I'll never be her, Kam. I'm nothing like her." Kendall sighed. She had spent so much time trying to be anything other than her sister, hoping she would get more attention from her parents. Any attention was better than being overshadowed by Hannah. A flower cannot grow in the shade of a mighty oak.

"I never wanted Hannah." His voice was soft and regretful. "If only I had."

"I don't understand." Kendall pushed off his lap and reached for her throw blanket to wrap around herself. "You want her, you don't want her. You don't make any sense, Kameron Knight."

"She used to call me Kameron when she was mad too. If only she had stayed that way."

Kendall saw the way he looked at the floor. He was filled with disgust...for himself? Kendall realized there was more to the story than he had previously shared. "What happened, Kam?"

"I fell in love with another. It broke her heart, and she...."

"You have to tell me, Kam." Kendall almost held her breath as she waited for his last words.

"It was my fault. If I hadn't broken her heart, she would have been more careful. She was distracted." His words were hollow.

"Is that what this is about?" Kendall shook her head at him.

"I didn't mean to hurt her."

"No, I imagine you didn't, but Hannah was a big girl, Kam. She was strong and smart. I guarantee she didn't let you distract her. Sometimes horrible things happen, things that are outside our control."

"But she—"

"Were you with her, Kam?" Kendall asked him quietly.

"No."

"Then you couldn't possibly know what happened. A life can end in one split second, Kam. From what we learned, the whole group was ambushed. Hannah helped get a few of them to safety. To me, that proves her head was on straight."

"She went back in, Kendall."

"Kameron Knight, tell me something. If you had a man down, would you go back in for them?"

"Yes, but—"

"There's no buts. Hannah was many things, but she was not a coward. Stop taking credit for her death. In doing so, you belittle everything she did the day she died," Kendall chastised him.

Kam sucked in his breath in surprise at her words. He looked as if he wanted to say something else, but thought better of it. Instead, his mouth opened in a relieved smile. "She always raved about how smart you were."

Kendall snorted. "She got the beauty and the brains, I'm afraid."

"Stop that." His voice was sharp.

"What? It's the truth. I hated school, and school hated me."

"Most people do. Some more than others. There must have been something you loved."

Dancing and you, she wanted to say, but instead, she turned away from him. Walking over to the window, she looked at the pitch-black skies outside. Hardly any stars were in the sky. "That was a lifetime ago. I think you should go, Kam."

"You're mad at me. Damn it."

"No, I'm a realist." She was too. Realistically, this would never work between them. She didn't want to be with someone who was with her out of guilt.

"What do you mean?"

"You're here out of guilt, Kam. I don't need your pity." Kendall sighed sadly.

"That's not why I'm here, Kendall."

Kendall knew he was trying to convince her, but his words fell short. "Then why are you here?"

She waited for him to answer her, but no words came. Turning around, she almost gasped when she saw the raw desire in his eyes. The liquid gold in his eyes had returned. Its heat was mesmerizing. Stepping closer to him, she reached out to touch him, but Kam stepped away before she could.

Tears filled her eyes. "Go, Kam."

"I can't...." His words were tortured.

"You can't go. You don't want to stay. I can't touch you." Kendall felt a fury rising inside her. "Get out!"

"If that's what you want," he answered softly.

She sniffed in irritation. "It doesn't matter what I want,

Kam. I can't compete with ghosts."

"Is that what you think?" He stepped closer to her.

Kendall stepped back with every step he took toward her. When her back pressed against the wall, she realized there was nowhere else to go. Looking away from him, she squeezed her eyes shut.

His hands pressed into the wall above her head as he leaned over to whisper in her ear. "Every inch of me wants to make you mine, Kendall."

She shivered against the heat of his words. His mouth ran kisses down her neck, and her breath caught in her throat, distracting her enough to drop the blanket she had wrapped around herself. Her breasts arched into his chest as he trailed kisses up her neck to her chin. One of his hands reached down and caressed her areola gently, which sprang to life the second he touched her. As his mouth moved to hers, Kendall wrapped her arms around his neck and brought him closer to her.

Kam was shaking when he finally broke the kiss. Raw desire covered his face as he tried to rein in his control. Kam pushed away from her. "I will not take advantage of you right now, Kendall."

"Why not?" she whispered.

He shuddered at her words. "You need to grieve, Kendall. The next step for us, it's finite. There will be no going back."

"I'm not afraid of you, Kam."

"Maybe you should be." Kam's eyes flashed with desire before he stepped out of the room.

Kendall almost raced after him. "Where are you going?"

"The couch," he answered her. He turned back and saw

her standing naked in the doorway. "Do us both a favor and lock your door."

Kendall sucked in her breath. His words were intended to scare her, but instead, she found herself curious as to what was going to happen next. Closing her door behind her, she slid against it and shivered. Who said chivalry was dead? She touched her fingers to her mouth and closed her eyes. Kendall longed to find strength in his arms. This wasn't grief making her feel wild and wicked. She had never felt this way for anyone. Perhaps it was time to push the limit. She smiled to herself as a plan formed in her head. She'd let him off the hook until after her mother's service, but after that, he was fair game.

CHAPTER 7

The next morning, Kendall crept quietly from her room. She walked to the couch where Kam was supposed to be sleeping and found a note. He had a family emergency and would be away for the next few days. He wanted her to call him when she had a chance.

"Chicken," she muttered. She crumpled the note up and tossed it in the trash. So much for her plans to make him get past his guilt to actually see her for what she was. His absence almost felt like a betrayal of the trust she had been too willing to give.

He had left the ball in her court, which she decided to just drop on the floor. She had too much to do to dwell over what he did or did not want from her. Kendall decided to do what she always did best—sink further into herself and forget the world around her. Let Kam figure out what he wanted from life—Kendall barely wanted to live it.

First, a day passed, then another. Kendall decided she could not wait for him to prove he really cared. She continued to put one foot in front of the other. This was just another reminder that the universe wanted her to be alone. Kendall did not have time for any games.

The weeks passed, and Kendall dealt with laying her mother to rest as well as packing up the rest of the house. All things she did on her own, as she did every other step in her life. If Kam had wanted to truly be there for her, he would have found a way. Instead, he was decisively absent. That spoke volumes in itself.

More time passed, and the house she had grown up in became someone else's forever home. Kendall had found herself a small cabin on the outskirts of town, which backed up to the forest behind her. With the money from the sale of the house and the inheritance she had received, Kendall decided to spend the time getting back to her basics. The nature around her was the perfect balm to her aching heart.

Her bitterness grew. He had told her she didn't have to be alone, yet here she was standing on the edge of a cliff that no one was able to talk her off of, a loneliness she would never be able to shake. That night the darkness ate at her heart in a way it never had, and she took it with her into the forest. Something was growing inside her, a need to break free from the shell she had built around her.

Kendall had not planned the interlude in the forest. She took her music with her to block out the eeriness of the world around her. When she found a clearing in the woods, Kendall sat down on the ground and looked up at the moon above her, full in all its glory. A soft glow filled the air around her. Closing her eyes, she turned up the volume on her headphones and breathed in the cool air around her.

It had been years since she had danced in the open air, something she had loved to do when she was a child. The soft ebb and flow of the music in her ears opened something she had buried deep inside her. Her arms flexed over her head as she felt each beat of the music pumping through her. A haunting melody carried her across the clearing like the white swan coming to life under the moonlight. Years fell away from her as she remembered what it was she had loved so much so long ago.

Dancing had been her passion until she entered her first year of high school. Due to dwindling grades, her parents had cut her lessons short. Kendall had never forgiven them for that. She could pinpoint the anger that boiled deep inside her to that one moment. Taking away what she loved had not made her any smarter. Kendall was not an honor student and had never planned on going to college. She never did, nor had she danced ever again.

Tears streamed down her face as she realized all the joy that had been missing from her life. Every leap, twist, and turn was filled with emotions that broke her into pieces that she could not pick up. As she danced, she was unaware of the eyes that watched her from the trees in the forest. She was oblivious to everything but the emotional dance that became a lyrical extension of herself.

As the song changed, she closed her eyes. Her mind turned to Kam, who had been a fantasy for far too long. Even though she was furious with him, she wanted him more than she could ever admit. The tempo of the song picked up, and she put every inch of her desire into her movements. Every movement was punctuated with a longing she could not voice. She had always been complimented for the way she showed her emotions through her dance.

When the song was over, Kendall was sitting on the

ground. She curled her knees into her chest and hugged them tight to her body. With her eyes closed, she imagined how his strength and warmth would feel if he were there with her. She wanted to curl up against him and lose herself in the comfort of his touch, but he wasn't there. Kendall felt tears fall down her face as she put her head against her knees.

"Don't cry, Kendall. I can't bear it." His voice was just a whisper on the breeze, so faint she was afraid she never heard it.

Pulling her earbuds out of her ears, she turned to find Kam standing behind her. "Go away, Kam."

"No." He refused.

"Why are you here?"

"The moonlight called me. I'm glad it did. Your sister used to talk about your dancing. She was right."

"About what?" Kendall crossed her arms over her chest as she stood up.

"You're exquisite."

Her eyes met his, and she shook her head. "Hannah never said that."

"Yes, she did. She was angry at your parents for making you give it up. They should never have done that."

"I'm used to disappointment by now." Kendall looked down at the ground, unable to meet his eyes any longer. She started to walk away from him.

"That last dance, Kendall. What was it about?" He put his hand on her shoulder, and she turned around to face him.

"Another time. Another place. It doesn't exist anymore."

She pulled away from him, trying her best to build a wall around herself. Her vulnerability was far too close to the surface. Every inch of her wanted to run into the safety of his arms, even if he faded away with the morning light.

"You never called me."

"You left," she accused him.

"I had to take care of some things."

"Good for you." Kendall sighed as she continued up the path that would lead her back to her cabin.

"I got called away, Kendall. You have to believe me." He stepped in front of her and held his hand up.

"I don't *have* to do anything. I can't believe I was trying to figure out how to seduce you. I must have lost my mind that night."

"Shit." He ran a hand through his hair. "Kendall, just give me a chance to explain."

"I needed you, Kam." Her voice was covered in pain.

He looked down at the ground. "You're right. I was afraid."

"Afraid? Of what?" Kendall wasn't even sure she would accept his explanation.

"That I would do something you would hate me for."

"I don't understand."

"Werewolves mate for life, Kendall. I can only have one mate. That woman will not be able to have any other man. That means whoever I choose will be stuck with me. If I had stayed, you would not have had a choice. My wolf was prepared to take it at all costs."

"And now?" she asked him curiously.

"Nothing has changed."

"I see." She nibbled on her bottom lip. "No, that's not true. I don't see. I don't understand how you felt it was easier to run away than it was to give me a fucking choice. Go to hell, Kameron Knight."

"I'm already there." His eyes were filled with a pain that Kendall recognized.

To be close to the only person that made her want to live was deadly. He had the ability to ruin everything she was. He had already destroyed the fantasies she had woven around her heart so long ago. "I hate you, Kam."

"Why?" Kam's eyes flashed golden fire as he steeled himself for her reply.

"Because you made me love you, and then you left." Tears fell down her face.

He stepped closer to her, and this time Kendall stood her ground. When his mouth slid over hers, she shivered against him. In a matter of seconds, it was as if no time had passed at all. Kendall closed her eyes and let herself imagine what it would be like to fall into his arms for the rest of her life. When he broke the kiss, she felt as if she had been missing him all her life.

Kam ran a hand through her hair. "You're so beautiful."

"So are you." Her voice was wistful.

At that moment, Kam's phone started to ring. He pulled it out of his pocket. "You've got to be fucking kidding me."

"It's okay. Go." Kendall stepped back from him with the worst form of déjà vu racing through her head.

"I don't want to leave you, Kendall," he called after her.

"And yet, you always do." She didn't even turn around to look at him. What was the point?

"Please let me explain." Kam's voice was haunted.

Kendall sighed and crossed her arms over her chest.

Turning around, she put her chin in the air. "Very well."

"There might be another murder."

"Excuse me?" Her eyebrows rose curiously.

"The first one happened that night. A ritual killing."

"Then why wasn't it on the news?" She challenged his story.

"Because no one cares about witches, Kendall. But we do. We do our best to protect the witch camp from the evil that haunts Witch's Hollow. That is our job."

"Prove it." Kendall let her hands slide down to her side.

"How?"

"Take me with you."

"It's not a sight you should see." Kam shook his head and waved her words away.

"I've seen more than you know, Kam. Maybe I can help."

This was not her first rodeo. Having been around enough evil to last a lifetime, Kendall was more than ready to offer her assistance. There was also a bigger part of herself that had to see it with her own eyes. She was having trust issues at the moment.

"I would, but there's a problem with that." Kam looked away from her.

"If you don't take me with you, Kameron Knight, I will walk out of your life forever." Kendall put her foot down. No more lies. If he wanted her in his life, he would have to find a way to put his worries behind him.

"You wouldn't."

"Don't be too sure of what I would or wouldn't do. You don't know me as well as you think you do. I'm not a child." Every inch of her was starting to get pissed off. Her hair rose in the air with a slight crackle as her anger came to the surface. Kendall was tired of people thinking they could make her decisions for her. Never again.

"No." Desire flashed in his eyes. "You're not a child."

"Then take me with you."

"My brothers.... They don't—"

"Know about me?" Kendall rolled her eyes and fought the urge to spit on the ground. Was he ashamed of her? Tears threatened to fall, and she realized that this was probably never going to work. Kam was holding himself back, and she was tired of fighting him for something he should want to give. Werewolf be damned. "Goodbye, Kam."

Shoving her earbuds in, Kendall cranked up her music as high as it would go. The emotions churning inside her were reckless. The last time she had felt this way, she had made one of the worst mistakes of her life, a mistake that still haunted her to this day. This anger had sent her into the arms of the one man who had no issues with ruining her innocence. Alistair had only cared about himself. She had thought that Kameron Knight was different. Apparently, they were all the same.

A roar erupted behind her, loud enough to break through the music she pumped into her ears. She pulled the earbuds out of her ears and turned to find Kam fighting something that he seemed incapable of controlling. He tossed his phone down to the ground and moved toward her.

The desire flashing through his eyes made her breath stop in her chest. His lips were on hers before she could ward him off. The desire rippled between them, and Kendall felt Kam pushing past the walls he had built around himself. His hands slid under her shirt as his tongue plundered the depths of her mouth.

He slid the shirt up her stomach, and she shivered in the cold night air. His mouth moved down her face, his beard scratching her flesh deliciously. His fingers unhooked her bra and shoved the straps from her shoulders. She felt his hands push under the bands of her leggings, and she trembled for his touch.

Before she knew it, she was naked in the moonlight, with the only man who had ever made her heart race like a raging machine. She heard the chime of his phone and heard him curse at it. Kendall sighed in disappointment. "You have to go."

"Like hell." He wrapped his hands in her hair and brought her closer to him.

Kendall had not realized that she was not the only one who was naked. She felt the heat of his skin sear her flesh as he held her against him. His mouth captured hers in a wild kiss that robbed her of all her sanity. The phone rang again, and Kam broke the kiss, tortured by the choices he had to make.

"I want to make you mine, Kendall. Screw that. I need to make you mine. I'll die without you." His eyes were fierce, changing from green to gold then back again.

"Do it," she told him. Kendall wasn't sure what it meant, only that they would be bound together for the rest of their lives. She was only half alive without him. No way did she want to go back to that life.

He growled and grabbed her ass. Hefting her legs into the air, he guided them behind him as he slid his swollen cock inside her. Kendall whimpered as his heat warmed her core.

When he moved slowly inside her, she shivered against him.

"God, you feel so tight," he groaned as he pumped into her. His mouth came down to her neck. "I don't want to hurt you," he whispered against her flesh. His movements slowed as he tried to keep something at bay.

Kendall realized the myths were true. A werewolf had to bite its mate to claim it. She wasn't afraid of it. Every inch of her craved it. She squeezed herself around his cock and tried to get him to move deep inside her. She had to build his frenzy to make him take action. Reaching up, she pulled his face down to her neck. "Please, Kam."

He trembled. The more she moved herself onto him, the harder it was for him to push his need aside. "Kendall...."

The phone rang again, and she felt him harden beneath her. Her nails made a trail down his back, and he tensed against her. Every inch of him was trying to ignore the need she felt in him. "Take me, Kam. Now."

He groaned against her and started to ram into her depths with a fever he could no longer ignore. His teeth sunk into her flesh and her breath caught in her throat. Every inch of her longed for so much more, but she knew that he was about to break. Wrapping her arms around his neck, she held on for the ride of her life. When his cock shuddered inside her, she felt a warm trickle slide down her legs.

Kam cursed under his breath as the phone rang again. "Damn it. This was not the way...."

Kendall unwound her legs and slid down the length of him. Laying her head on his chest, she felt more connected to him than any other being on the planet. He might leave her now, but this time he had to come back. She had cemented her place in his life by forcing his hand. She should feel guilty, but she didn't. Not one bit.

Kam put a hand under her chin and forced her to look into his eyes. "I have to help them, Kendall."

"I know."

"I don't want to go." His lips trailed a soft path to her ear, and his hot breath tickled her skin. "The next time I take you, you'll be screaming my name."

Kendall felt her nipples harden against his chest. "I'll be waiting. You know where to find me."

Kendall reached down and scooped up her clothes, and watched him walk across the clearing in all his naked glory. Every inch of him was chiseled with muscles that did not seem to stop. She remembered the way his skin felt against hers, and she closed her eyes.

"Stop it, Kendall."

Her eyes flew open. "What?"

"If you continue to think about me that way, I'll never be able to concentrate." He grinned at her, but the seriousness behind his words was etched in every inch of his eyes.

She snorted as she put her clothes back on. "Good luck with that."

He shook his head as he put his clothes back on. She watched in a trance as he shifted into his wolf right in front of her. Her breath caught in her throat, and she smiled at him.

"Go. The faster you leave, the easier it will be to return to me."

Kendall waved him off and sighed to herself. Life had certainly changed in ways she had never expected. She put her headphones in her ears and hummed along with the music as she headed back to her cabin. For once, she had not a care in the world.

CHAPTER 8

Kam raced through the forest, his emotions raw and confused. When he made it to his brothers, he was not prepared to deal with them. Not that they had any clue how to not meddle in his business.

"What the hell took you so long?" Karter almost shouted at him.

"Heaven forbid I actually had something else that I needed to do," Kam almost snarled.

"Oh shit, don't ruffle his feathers," cautioned Kyle.

"Why not?" Karter asked curiously.

"Because you fucked up my night." Kam put his fists at his sides and clenched them so tight he nearly drew blood from his nails. He had not planned to take Kendall so forcefully, but he was afraid if he didn't do it then, she would run from his life for the last time.

Killian walked around him and sniffed the air. "Shit. You finally did it."

"Did what?" Kyle's eyes narrowed on Kam.

"You're right. He did." Karter grinned at Kam. "About time."

Kyle still had a clueless look plastered on his face. "What

69

did you do?"

"He took a mate. You'd know about that if you actually kept your dick in your pants long enough to sniff out your own mate," Karter chuckled.

Kyle rolled his eyes. "So, I'm not in a hurry. What's it to you?"

"So, who is she?" Karter nudged his brother with his elbow.

"None of your damn business." Kam was not ready to share her with the rest of his family. They could be overbearing and obnoxious. With everything she had been through lately, bringing her into his world would be something he had to do one step at a time.

"Don't let Mother hear about this," cautioned Kyle. "You know she'll want to meet her. It is a her, right?"

"Fuck you!" Kam growled at his brother.

"Such language," teased Kyle.

Killian put an arm around Kam just before he tried to launch himself at their younger brother. "Just think, now that you've found your mate, we can spend all our time giving this one grief."

Kam smirked and relaxed in his brother's hold. "You're right."

"Whatever." Kyle shook off their words.

"So, what are we here for?" asked Kam. "Did you find a body?"

"No, but we found more blood. It's not from any animal, either."

Kam sniffed the air and could almost taste the blood that tainted the air. Human blood. Enough to capture their attention, but not quite enough to imply a death had happened. "So, what's the plan?"

"We need to figure out what is happening at the altar."

"How are we going to do that? The dark casters seem to disappear whenever we're around." Kyle gestured to the empty table stone in the middle of Witch's Hollow.

"I think that's the point." Kam looked over to Killian. "So, we're doing this in shifts?"

"There are four of us here. Five whenever Kendrick brings his ass home. I don't think we should do solo shifts." Killian ran a hand through his hair. "We have to put a stop to this. They need to know we won't accept their interference here."

"Are we even sure it's the regulars?" Kam asked him. For the most part, the dark casters nearby knew their limitations. Kam may not agree with their belief system, but they had as much right to be here as anyone else. As long as they respected the life around them, that was.

"I'm not sure who or what it is." Killian was looking out in the distance, with a fear that was reflected on Karter's face.

"Don't worry. We'll keep them all safe," Kam assured his brothers. Now that he had mated, he understood the fierce need to protect the women in their lives. If anyone thought of putting a hand on Kendall, he would rip it directly from their bodies.

"The last time this happened...." Karter clamped his mouth shut.

"It's not going to—" A loud scream interrupted him, one that came from somewhere in the distance. He recognized it, and fear erupted around him. "Kendall."

"Who is Kendall?" Kyle asked curiously as he turned to

71

the sound of the scream.

"No time for that." Kam shifted into Kiego and bolted toward the sounds of the only living soul who mattered to him at that moment in time. *Please let her be all right.* He begged the universe. He had just claimed her. If he lost her now, he would never forgive himself.

The land seemed to blur around him. He ignored the wolves that were flying fast behind him. When he found her, he breathed a sigh of relief. She was kneeling on the ground over a woman's body, her mouth uttering words he could not understand, but it sounded like a prayer of cleansing. The others were right behind him. Kam returned to his human shape and put his hand on her shoulder.

Kendall jumped and almost rammed her fist into his face. When she realized who it was, she threw herself into his arms. "Kam!"

"Shhh.... It's okay, Kendall."

"But it's not. This is all my fault." She wept into his shoulder, pitiful wails that tore him into millions of pieces.

"It's not your fault, Kendall." He soothed her with his words, aware of the brothers who were standing around them.

Her eyes flew open as she saw the tall men staring at them with a sense of almost shock. "Oh.... Um...Kam?"

"Yes?" Sensing her concern, Kam looked around at his brothers. He let out a disgusted sigh. "These idiots seem to follow me everywhere. Kendall, meet my brothers."

Kendall pushed away from Kam and stood up to face them. Her eyes leveled on each and every one of them, and Kam took pleasure in the way they seemed to look away from her appraisal. Kendall was a lot of things, but a coward was not one of them.

"And you are?" she grilled each and every one of them.

"Killian." Killian grimaced slightly.

"Karter." Karter had a merry twinkle to his eyes, and when he turned to look at Kam, he gave him a thumbs up.

"And you?"

Kyle had refused to answer. His mouth was still wide open. "Oh...uhm...Kyle. Kam never told us how—"

"Young I am?" she offered.

"Um, well—"

"Shut it," warned Kam. He did not need his brother spilling any of the beans. Kyle had been the only one to have seen the picture of Kendall. He had caught Kam doing something no brother should walk in on.

Kyle gave him a wry smile. "Pleased to meet you. Kam has—"

"Kyle," growled Kam.

"Not told us a thing about you, unfortunately."

"I can see why." Kendall snorted at him. "You're a little immature, aren't you?"

Kam puffed his chest out as he saw the way Kendall cut Kyle down to size. Immature was just one word to describe him. Several came to mind, but now was not the time.

"You were saying you thought this was your fault." Killian interrupted the moment.

Kendall's eyes now looked haunted. "I recognize the work." Reaching down, Kendall pulled the shirt up to where a few symbols had been carved into the woman's flesh. She looked up at Kam with self-loathing plastered on her face.

"It's Alistair's work."

Kam growled before he could stop himself. He saw the fear pass over Kendall's face and instantly regretted it. His face softened, and he tried to comfort her, but Kendall inched away from his touch.

"Why is he here?" Killian asked her.

"He knows I'm here." A tear fell down her face, and Kam had to stop himself from wiping it away.

"What do you mean?" Karter asked her.

Kendall looked down at the ground. Her fear was palpable when she spoke next. "For years, he kept me imprisoned in his dungeon. I've seen things I wish I could forget. They're tattooed on my brain in ways I can never explain."

Kam saw her grab her stomach and wondered what that asshole had done to her so long ago. He sensed there was more to the story, but now was not the time to press it. "We've never seen her before."

"Her name's Ilah. She was there too." Shadows crossed her face, and Kam knew she was trapped in a personal hell that he wanted to pull her out of.

"How many women does he keep?"

"Sometimes four, always three. We were all expendable." She held up her arm and showed a small scar near her wrist. "He likes to bleed us, take us to the brink of death, and remind us that he has control over us."

Kam roared in anger. "I'll kill him."

"Not if I get to him first," promised Kendall.

The men turned to stare at the witch that stood before them. Gone was the fear that had been there moments before. A red glow surrounded her as her anger rose to the surface.

Like a flame, it ebbed dangerously.

"Shit." Kyle stepped back slightly. "Can I get me one of those?"

Kam reached his fist back to slam it into Kyle's face, but Karter caught it midair with his own. "Let me kill him. We still have another brother."

Kyle stepped in front of him and nodded his head. Then he pounded his fist to his chest. "Bring it. I'm not afraid of you."

Kendall's hair rose in the air as her annoyance crackled around her. "Seriously? You're going to fight at a time like this? Assholes."

Kendall's fiery shield subsided, and she shook her head before she knelt down next to Ilah's body. Magic flowed from her hands as she attempted to close the wounds in an effort to remove the symbols. When they would not seal, she slammed her fist into the ground. "I should have killed him when I had the chance."

"Kendall, we need to take her body." Killian knelt beside her. "We'll take her to the witch's camp. They'll help her soul pass to the next life."

Kendall nodded her head and sighed softly. She put a hand on her friend, and a tear fell down her face. "I'm so sorry, Ilah."

Kam touched his hand to her face. "Kendall...."

She looked up at him. "Be careful with her."

"I'll be there soon." Kam saw the mournful smile that reflected back at him.

"I should have let you go."

Kam sucked in his breath. Was she regretting her choice?

His brothers had the decency to step away, but he knew they would hear her answer. "Why, Kendall?"

"Now, you're stuck with me."

He breathed a sigh of relief. "Is that all?"

She looked confused at his reply. "One day you'll—"

"No, I won't," he promised her. "Now, get your ass home and lock the doors, Kendall."

"But—"

"Just do it, Kendall."

Anger flashed in his eyes. Everything about her frustrated the hell out of him. He wanted to shake some sense into her, but right now, her mind was not in the right place, and he had to get to the bottom of whatever was happening in Witch's Hollow, whether that meant Alistair was involved or not. If that man were smart, he would go deep into hiding. Never mess with a wolf's mate. This was not going to go well for him at all, especially if Alistair ever laid another hand on her. His brethren were tightly knit. Mess with one of their mates, and you messed with all of them. That man's time was limited. That was a guarantee.

CHAPTER 9

Kendall was beside herself with grief by the time she made it back to her cabin. Locking the door behind her, she curled up on the couch and let her sadness cover her like a blanket. The life she had left behind was one she had been trying to fight against. Kendall had thought if she shut out the voices in her head that they would cease to exist.

Closing her eyes, she saw the torture chamber in her mind as if she were still trapped inside it. The flick of the whip across her flesh as Alistair tried to mold her to his will. He never struck her hard enough to leave a mark, but the pain had still been excruciating. The memories tortured her all over again.

How she could have fallen for such a cruel, manipulative bastard, she would never understand. At first, he had deceived her into thinking he was a gentleman. She had been naive, a teenager rebelling against the world her parents kept her stifled inside. Kendall had snuck out any chance she could, entering a world darker than her own. His control over her had saturated every inch of her life. The minute she was old enough to leave, Kendall had picked up and walked away from everyone who had ever loved her.

Tears fell down her face as she remembered how much

pain she had caused her parents over that asshole. They had never met Alistair, never knew the lengths to which he would go to keep her by his side. Kendall was desperate for love, starving for a taste of something that would take the sorrow away.

Hannah's death had hit her hard. She had been filled with guilt for fantasizing over the man her sister had fallen in love with. Alistair had replaced her fantasy crush with a nightmare that still scarred her memories. She glanced down at the small circles that were unnoticeable to anyone who didn't know the story. Running her nails against them, she fought the urge to erase them entirely by ripping them open and letting the darkness drain out of her.

Squeezing her hands into fists, she tried to pull herself together. Reining in her thoughts, she reminded herself that she had tried to get the others to come with her. She had even made a report to the authorities, which they had brushed aside like she was crazy. Perhaps she had been hysterical when she walked into the police station, but that did not mean they should have disregarded her. It was as Kam had said before—no one cared about the witches of the world. Law enforcement turned their eyes with their self-satisfied smiles any time one of the occult was killed. Witches were not dirty creatures to be cast aside. They were living, breathing human beings. The fact that they got lumped in with Satanists was completely illogical. Witches upheld life and paid homage to all the energy that swirled in the open air around them. They cared more about the state of the world than most people. Just because their beliefs did not fit into some cookie cutter religion did not make them bad people, but that didn't really matter to anyone outside their belief system.

That was life, though, the one she had become accustomed to. Had she known that the deaths in the hollow were related to Alistair, she would have done something earlier. She could not sit there and do nothing. If Kam thought he could shelf her when she could help track that bastard down, he had another thing coming. She would not rest until they had erased his narrative from this planet.

A knock sounded on the door, and Kendall nearly jumped out of her socks. She left the couch and walked slowly to the door, almost afraid to see what might be on the other side. The knock sounded again.

"You can open the door, Kendall." Kam's gruff voice echoed through the wood.

"Thank goodness!" She unlatched the lock and pulled the door open. Kendall threw herself into his arms and breathed in his earthy scent.

Kam chuckled softly. "It's good to see you too."

He closed the door behind him and reached his hand up to lock the door. Kendall's tears started to flow against her will. Kam held her tightly against him and soothed her as his hands stroked her back softly. "Let it out, Kendall. I've got you."

Kendall couldn't have stopped the tears if she'd wanted to. Seeing Ilah there on the cold ground was something she would never forget. She hadn't known her that well, only that Ilah had been there long before she had. The witch had very little to say to the rest of them. She was probably the one that was most loyal to Alistair. Kendall was actually lucky that Ilah hadn't sounded the alarm when she escaped.

"Tell me about him, Kendall." Kam's voice was gruff with emotion.

"You don't want to know, Kam." She shivered as haunting memories rose to the surface.

"If it happened to you, then I need to know, Kendall. I can't pretend this man never hurt you. I refuse to stay in the dark."

Kendall sighed. "Fine. Have a seat." Kendall was relieved when he chose the love seat across from the couch. If he sat next to her, she would never get through it. "Where do you want me to start, Kam?"

"Try the beginning."

"Hannah died. I was so lost without her, and I felt sick inside."

"Why?" he asked her quietly.

"Because I was so jealous of her. She had what I wanted. I thought she had you."

He smiled softly at her. "Jealousy will eat the soul. The very thought of any other man touching you destroys me."

"Then, you don't need to hear about him, Kam."

"Yes. I do." His eyes probed hers. "Your pain is my pain, Kendall."

She looked away from him. If he watched her through all of this, she would never be able to get through it. "I snuck out to a club with one of my friends. When I met Alistair there, I was flattered by his attention. And incredibly naïve. Sarah tried to talk me out of it, but I left the club with him. That night...well, I was never the same after."

"What did he do?" Kam's voice told her that he would not back down from her.

"Took me to his apartment and plied me with drinks that had a bizarre taste to them. When I woke up the next morning, I was naked in his bed."

"Asshole."

"I don't remember much from that night really, but the way he treated me after made me think I had enjoyed the experience." Kendall sighed. "It took me years to figure out that had been a lie. That wasn't the only time he raped me. There were too many times to count. Each time, he made me feel like I had asked for it. I was too ashamed of the woman I had become to go home."

"How does dark magic come into it?"

"He used it to control me. Like an imaginary chain, he kept me tethered to his side. Draining the life from me one drop at a time. His dark magic seemed to course through my veins. It took me some time to realize that was not what I was feeling. It wasn't my blood he was trying to take. It was my magic."

"You're not a dark caster, Kendall. Anyone with eyes can see that."

"I believed whatever he wanted me to believe until the truth of his actions started to bleed through my mind. That's when I started to hone my craft in my own time. When I was able to control the energy that cycled through me, I made a plan to escape his horrible clutches. I tried to get them to leave with me, but they had been bound to him for much longer than I had." Her eyes met his briefly before shame filled her. She looked down to the ground, and a tear slid down her face. "You should have picked someone else."

"No one else exists for me, whether I claimed you or not,

Kendall."

"What if I can't give you what you want?" She whispered.

"What is it that you think I want, Kendall?" He knelt before her and stroked her face with his hands.

"A family." She took his hand in hers and moved it to her stomach. "He...oh god, how do I even begin? I'm horribly scarred, Kam. His rituals, they were—"

"Don't finish that," he whispered as he pulled her into his arms. He kissed the top of her forehead as the tears started to fall.

Before she knew it, she was sobbing uncontrollably, as she had never realized how much she wanted a child of her own. She never thought she would find a man that made her want them. Now, the very idea that they might not even be an option broke her heart.

Kam rocked her in his arms and soothed her like a long lost child. "I have everything I want here in my arms, Kendall."

"What if I'm not enough?" she whispered.

"You're all I ever wanted, Kendall. The moment you chose me, my life was complete." His mouth came down to hers and soothed the rest of her sorrow away before she could object.

When he broke the kiss, she sighed against him. "So... your brothers must have their opinions about us."

"I think Kyle's got a crush on you already," he chuckled.

Kendall slapped his arm. "Stop!"

"No, it's true. He's going to be hard to live with. Only one thing we can do about that."

"What's that?" Kendall wondered aloud.

"Find him his own mate to tend to."

"Oh? And just what is involved in this tending?" Her curiosity was piqued.

"A little of this...." He trailed soft kisses across her face, making a path to her ear, where he nibbled on the bottom of her lobe. "And a little of that."

"Oh. And if that's not enough?" She teased him.

"Don't worry, I have a whole basket of tricks."

"Really? Do tell."

Kendall reached around his neck and pulled him closer to her. Her tongue licked the outside of his mouth, and she sighed when he sucked it into his mouth. His tongue battled for control over hers, and Kendall was happy to yield to it. She was so distracted by him, she didn't realize he had lifted her into the air.

She broke the kiss. "Where are you taking me?"

"To bed." His eyes flashed with desire.

"How do you know where it is?"

"Truth?"

"Yes, Kameron. The truth."

"It used to be my cabin." He grinned at her.

"How did you know I would buy it?"

"I didn't, but I hoped you would."

"Where do you live?" she asked him.

"I'm in between places." He chuckled when she hit his chest with her fists.

"Kameron Knight!" She couldn't believe he had done that. Stroking his face with her hand, she looked into his eyes and got lost in their depths. "This is your home, Kam."

"It is your home." He laid her down on the bed and crawled over her.

She ran a hand against the scruff on his face. "Not without you, it's not."

"Kendall—"

"Say you'll stay...." She wanted to beg him to never leave her again, but Kendall could not bear to hear him promise something he would not be able to keep.

"I'm not going anywhere, Kendall."

"What if—?"

"I turned my phone off, Kendall. Tonight, there's only you." He kissed her forehead. "And me." He trailed kisses down her neck until she arched against him. "And this."

"Promise?" she whispered. She wanted him to rewrite the narrative in her head, to prove that there was more to sex than a carnal desire. Her brief interlude in the forest with him had barely given her any insight. It was a means to an end at that point, a way to tie him to her for the rest of her life. It was probably the most selfish thing she had ever done in her life.

"I plan to take my time, Kendall."

She shivered under him, wondering just how much time that would be. He slid his hands under her shirt, and her skin trembled under his touch. He slid the shirt up her back, and she helped him get it over her head.

"My turn," she whispered. Kendall's fingers touched the muscles of his stomach, reveling in the way they bunched up under her touch. Her lips sought his as she pushed the shirt upward. She only broke the kiss long enough to get the shirt over his head. She giggled when he tossed it far away from him.

"Are you laughing at me, woman?" His voice was gruff.

"Yes." She rubbed her finger along the scruff on his chin.

"You'll pay for that," he teased her.

"Oh?" She wondered what he had in mind, but she did not have to wonder long as his mouth bit her nipple through the lace of her bra. Her insides ignited, and she gasped when he tugged her nipple gently forward.

He let her go and licked the valley of her breasts like it was a delicious dessert. His hands slid down and pushed against the elastic bands holding her leggings in place. She thought he was going to remove them, but instead, his fingers slid down between her legs to stroke against her. Kendall nearly bucked off the bed. No one had ever touched her like that. Alistair had not been one to give any pleasure to his women, only took what he wanted or forced them to do all the work.

"Look at me, Kendall."

Her eyes snapped open, and she gazed into his misty depths. He was willing her to stay in the moment. His finger moved soft and slow over her clit. A warm light started to glow in the pit of her stomach as delicious desire grew to a feverish peak. She leaned her head back and closed her eyes.

"Look at me, Kendall. I want to see you when you cum against me."

Her breath caught in her throat, and she almost wet herself at his words. She looked into his eyes, afraid she would incinerate under his touch. While she had never had a man make her orgasm, she had managed to manipulate her own, usually after fantasizing about this very moment with the man of her dreams. Remembering the way she had writhed beneath her sheets in her hot wet teenage dreams made her cum hard against his hand.

Kam swallowed her moans with his mouth as he shoved

his tongue into hers. The distraction made it hard to focus on the beautiful aftermath of her orgasm. She wanted to dwell in the moment, but he pushed through it with a frenzy that sent her over the edge. His fingers gave her no reprieve as they stroked her harder and faster, sending her well over the finish line.

He growled into her mouth, and she sucked his tongue hard inside it. Removing his hand, Kam slid down the length of her body, nibbling and kissing her flesh along the way. She trembled beneath him, unable to cool the currents that set her body on fire. He pulled her bottoms off and tossed them to the floor carelessly. Sliding her legs open, Kam positioned himself between her legs.

"What are you...? Ooh...."

Her stomach clenched as Kam's tongue pressed against her. He lapped at her juices as if he were starving for her flesh. When he sucked her clit into his mouth and nibbled gently, Kendall could not control the frenzy ripping through her. Her hips gyrated beneath him as she rode the wave he created. The faster she moved, the more his desire grew. He pushed her legs further apart and slid one of his fingers inside her.

"Oh!" Kendall was about to lose her mind. She shivered against him as another orgasm took her breath away. "Please, Kam."

He licked her and pulled away from her. "What do you want?"

"I want...." She didn't know how to ask for it. She never really had. It had never been something she chose.

He slid up the length of her body and stroked her face. "Tell me."

"I need you, Kam." Her eyes begged him not to make her say it.

"As you wish." He nuzzled her nose with his and slid to her neck. He licked her bite mark from earlier and moved up to her ear. "You're so wet. I'm not sure I could have held back much longer."

She whimpered as he slid into her. He was silky smooth inside her. The heat of his cock seared her insides, making her wild with longing. When he moved slowly, she felt like he was holding back. She wanted him to feel the same frenzied heat that she felt deep inside. Wrapping her legs around his ass, she pulled him in deeper.

He groaned, and she felt him tremble against her. "Slow down, Kendall."

"I can't help it," she gasped as he pushed into her further than before. A trembling started in the pit of her stomach, followed by a juicy release as she came all over him. She felt his stomach clench as she quivered around his cock.

"I've wanted this for far too long." He was still trying to hold himself back.

"Take me, Kam," her voice ordered him.

He growled, and his eyes flashed to a shade of gold that told her she was about to have the ride of her life. He thrust fast and hard as he took her over and over. When he could contain himself no longer, Kam plunged into her one last time, and a howl of release erupted around the room.

Kam rolled off her and fell against the bed. He wrapped his strong arms around her and pulled her against him. "You drive me crazy, Kendall Pearson."

"The feeling is mutual, Kameron Knight." She licked the

nipple that was close to her mouth and reveled in the way his breath caught in his chest.

"Kendall...," he warned her.

"What?" she asked him innocently.

"Time for a break, love."

"Fine," she grumbled and slid against him. She ignored his amused chuckle and closed her eyes. He was right. The minute she closed her eyes, she felt herself slipping into the after coma of a well-loved woman. She felt the covers slide over her as he adjusted against her. Kendall held him tight against her, half afraid when she woke up he would be just another torturous dream that teased her painfully.

CHAPTER 10

As the light of morning filtered in through the windows, Kendall stretched her arms and legs deliciously. When an arm slipped around her, she felt Kam's heat against her, and she sighed. For the first time in forever, Kendall's dreams had been non-existent. It was the most peaceful sleep she'd had in a long time. Most of the time her dreams were more nightmare than rainbows and moonbeams. It was a narrative that had been controlled by the experiences she'd had at Alistair's cruel hands.

Soft lips tickled her shoulders as Kam's hands massaged the skin at her navel. When he kissed the back of her neck, she felt a tremor of excitement ripple through her. His hand moved up and caressed her breast. Kendall whimpered when his fingers flicked against her nipple, which had decided to stand up and salute his attentions.

Kendall slid back against him and felt the heat of his flesh scar her own with a delicious need that grew inside her so easily. She had never felt so awake and alive before. Kam was a master of self-control, for a while she felt his swollen cock against her leg, he was more determined to give her satisfaction than to take what he needed.

"So soft," he whispered against her ear. He slid his hand between her legs and groaned. "And so wet."

Kendall moaned when his fingers started to stroke against her clit. He slid his other hand under her so he could stroke her other nipple while he kissed the back of her neck. Kendall had trouble focusing on one thing at a time. The combination of his movements made her ache for him. When she gyrated her hips, her ass rubbed against his erection, and she trembled against him with a need that scared her. The more his fingers stroked her, the more she pushed against him. When he started to push against her, rocking his cock in slow strokes against her cheek, she lost control.

"Oh...," she moaned against him as her body came undone against his fingers.

"That's it, baby. Let it all out."

"Gahhh!" Her toes curled as another orgasm followed the first. His fingers pinched her nipple tightly, and she groaned.

"There's more in there, Kendall. Cum for me." His hot breath on her ear sent her into a frenzy. Her hips pushed forward, and she rode against his fingers. She wanted to feel him deep inside her, taking every inch of her to a whole new world with him. Every journey to ecstasy was better than the last. Kendall wasn't sure how much more of this she could take.

When Kam lifted her leg and pushed inside her, she was more than ready for him. The slow rhythm he set was tantalizing. At first, she thought he was teasing her, but it became clear that he was prolonging his own release. She squeezed around him, and he flicked her nipple softly with his fingers.

"You feel so good, Kendall."

She shivered against him as his words set her on fire. Kendall locked her leg against his and arched her back. His hand slid around her and slipped between her legs. He stroked her clit, all the while continuing to take her slowly. When she came hard against him, he bit her shoulder blade and growled.

Sensing his restraint fading fast, she smiled to herself. She wanted him as wild as she was. As she squeezed against him, her silky wall pulled him in tight. A deep trembling started, one she could not seem to stop. Her breath was hard to control as he let go of his control. He rocked into her like a jackhammer, taking every inch of her with the length of his hard cock.

"Yes, oh, yes!" Kam's words forced their way out as if he were clenching his teeth together.

Her breath caught in her throat as he slammed into her one last time. She trembled over him as he released himself inside her. She had never felt so delicious in her entire life.

After, they lay there without speaking. The moment did not seem to require words. Kam kissed her shoulders while his hand stroked against her stomach. Her skin shivered beneath his touch. He pulled out of her and gathered her close to his body.

"Good morning, beautiful," he whispered in her ear.

"Yes, it is, isn't it?" She sighed against him.

"Any morning I wake up next to you is divine, Kendall." His fingers ran down her arm as he kissed below her ear.

Kendall turned in his arms and kissed his lips. "Where have you been all my life, Kameron Knight?"

"Right here waiting for you." He stroked her hair, and she smiled.

"I love you, Kam." Kendall nuzzled against his scruff and sighed.

"I love you too, Kendall." He kissed her and stroked the side of her face.

Kendall snuggled against him, trying to shut any dark thoughts out of the moment. Unfortunately, they had a nasty habit of rearing their ugly heads. She thought of her sister and how much she had cared for Kam. Would she forgive her for falling head over heels for him? She liked to think she would accept it if she were here. But then again, Kendall would never have instigated any of this if she had been. Should the sister code exist after death?

He stroked her cheek. "Stay in the moment, Kendall."

She blushed guiltily. "Sorry. I just —"

"She would be happy for us, Kendall." He kissed her forehead.

"Good, because I don't plan on giving you up any time soon." She snuggled against him.

"You couldn't if you tried. Unfortunately, I do have to get up. I promised to check in this morning."

"I understand." She smiled up at him, hoping she didn't look like a love-sick puppy.

"You can come with me if you like," he suggested.

"Are you sure?" Kendall nibbled on her bottom lip. After what she had shared about herself last night, she was afraid of what his brothers might think. Would they hold her past against her? Not that Kendall would blame them if they did.

Her mind turned back to the time when Alistair had

woven his spell around her. He had taken so much of her life from her. The old tenant building had been nearly deserted. Alistair had been a slum lord to the lowest sort, people who were just like him. The dark casters were more than people who manipulated magic. They had also created new street drugs that put unsuspecting people under psychotic trances, making them create a world of violence and fear wherever they roamed. And if that weren't bad enough, they fed from the innocent, controlling them to the point where their addictions made them easy to break. Feeding on their life and blood like vampires, these men were a darker breed of evil.

While she had managed to escape, sometimes she wondered how much of herself was still intact. Her innocence had been taken so easily, it was almost as if it had never existed. All that had been left was a fierce need to survive and find a way to release herself from the personal hell he had kept her in. She remembered the cold, lightless basement fashioned into a modern day dungeon. Instead of bars, there were chain link cages that were kept locked any time someone showed any sense of rebellion. Often they were removed completely. No one really knew what became of those women, but Kendall had a pretty good idea.

Kendall wondered why he had come here. Rainier was far from where Alistair had made his base. At times she had wondered if he had more than one place established. Was he taking over the area here? Manipulating the dark casters that had made Witch's Hollow their feeding grounds? She shivered against Kam, and he held her closer.

"What's going on in that head of yours, Kendall?"

"It's not worth repeating." She closed her eyes and prayed

that he left it at that.

"You can tell me anything, Kendall. You'll find I'm a good listener."

"I'm just trying to figure out why Alistair is here." She prayed it wasn't because he had lost sight of her. Just like Esme had said, as soon as her mother passed, he would find her. Perhaps she should visit the fortune teller again. Maybe she had more information for her that would be helpful to her situation.

"You're worried," Kam surmised.

"Yes. I hope I didn't bring him here." She sighed. "I had cast a binding spell to keep him away from me. I think it faded the moment my mother died."

"That's possible, but I think that would mean he was already in the area, Kendall. It's not like he teleported here." He rubbed his hand against her cheek. "I'm pretty sure this is not your fault. You did not create that man."

"No, but I didn't stop him."

"Don't worry, Kendall. We'll put an end to him," Kam promised her.

"As long as you don't think you're leaving me out." She held her chin up and waited for his argument.

"I don't think I could. You'd just go after him on your own. Best to keep my eyes on you, I think." He grinned at her.

"Seriously? You do know I can take care of myself, right?" Kendall rolled her eyes and clenched her teeth.

"I never said you couldn't. I know plenty of strong witches. My mother's one of them." He grinned at her. "I know better than to mess with her."

Her heart sunk to the bottom of her stomach. Would

his mother hate her? What if she heard about her time with Alistair? It was bad enough that she had shared it with Kam. She couldn't bear to think someone would judge her based on the choices she had made when she was hurt and confused.

"Don't worry, Kendall. She'll love you. Besides, Brina already did the lay work for all of the rest of us. Mother has mellowed out quite a bit since then. Although she does have a thing about blondes."

"Kameron Knight...." She gritted her teeth. "That's not very helpful."

"I'm kidding. She's going to love you, just as much as I do."

Kendall sighed. Her mind turned over inside itself, reminding her of all the things she may never be. Would his mother accept her if she knew she might never be able to give Kam the children he deserved? Kendall was still young, but she wasn't opposed to starting a family. She just never thought it would be an option. It still wasn't. Her mind turned back to the ritualistic ceremonies that Alistair had performed on her, and she sucked in her breath. She could smell the searing flesh even now.

"Where did you go, Kendall?" His eyes were filled with deep concern.

"There are so many things, Kam. I thought I had a handle on them, but these deaths have brought up the demons I had kept buried deep inside me."

"One day at a time, Kendall. One demon at a time."

Kendall thought of the photo she carried with her in her purse, reminding herself that not all of her memories were filled with dangerous men. There had always been that one who had haunted her from afar, with his calm green eyes that had called to her through a piece of paper. She smiled and nodded her head. "One demon at a time."

"Good. Time to get up."

"Do we have time for a shower?" Kendall asked him as she sat up.

Kam looked thoughtful. "You better take one without me."

"Why's that?" she asked curiously.

"If I get in there with you, we're not coming out for a long time." His grin lit up his face all the way to his sparkling green eyes.

She blushed as she thought about his words. He was probably right. "Rain check?"

"You can count on it."

Kendall felt his eyes on her as she walked across the room, naked as the day she was born. Usually, she would have felt self-conscious, but the way Kam looked at her made her feel like the most beautiful woman in the world. She made her way into the bathroom and turned the water on. Just as she slid under the stream, she heard his footsteps behind her. Turning around, she grinned at him.

"Took you long enough."

Kam's eyes were almost glowing with a gold light. "Apparently, neither one of us wants to let you out of our sight."

"Well, get in here before the water gets cold."

"We couldn't have that, now could we?" He moved into the stall and pulled her against him.

She felt his erection and gasped. "How in the world are

you still —?"

"It's been a really long time for both of us," he murmured as his mouth captured her breast in his mouth.

"How long?" Kendall wondered aloud.

"Years...." He nibbled on her areola, and Kendall wrapped her arms around his neck to steady herself.

"That sounds painful," she whispered.

"You have no idea...."

"My poor, sweet, Kam. Let me take care of you, love."

She found the bar of soap and made a lather in her hands. She ran her hands along his chest, flicking his nipples with her nails. When his eyes turned golden, she knew she had engaged the beast inside. Kendall wanted to take care of both of them. From what she understood, this was the only way his wolf could meld with her, through his human form.

Kendall brought her mouth up to his and licked the outside of his lips. She slid her hand down his body and made a soapy trail. Lathering up more soap in her hands, she ran her fingers over his erection, enjoying the silky smooth skin at the tip. Kam groaned against her mouth.

"Do you like that?" She asked when she broke away from the kiss.

"Yes, definitely."

"What if I...?" Kendall slid down to her knees slowly and licked the tip of his cock. It seemed to spring even further into life with a small flick as Kam's stomach muscles clenched. She heard him moan above her and took that as a sign that he had indeed enjoyed that. Swirling her tongue around the length of him, she tasted every inch. When she took him into her mouth, she thought he was going to fall over on the spot.

"God, Kendall...that is divine."

She shivered at his encouragement as she sucked him hard into her mouth. She reached around and grabbed his ass with her hands and squeezed his muscles tight. He clenched them as he growled in desire above her.

"If you keep that up, there won't be any left for you," he warned her.

Good, she thought to herself. She wanted to please him the way he had pleased her, with little thought to her own personal enjoyment. This was about making him understand how he made her feel any time she was around him. Kendall wanted every inch of him. She brought him as far into her mouth as she could, teasing him with her tongue all the way. Swirling her tongue around his shaft, she felt a desire ripple through her. Kendall wanted to suck him dry.

"Mmmm....that feels so good." Kam started to pump into her mouth, his desire climbing even higher.

Kendall reached her hand down and squeezed his ball sack in her fingers. She felt him shake against her mouth as he continued to push into her. The control she wielded over him was a power unlike any other, a power she was not going to relinquish any time soon. When she felt the warm trickle in her mouth, she sucked him harder.

"Oh...." His ass shook in her hands as his orgasm came to an end.

When she released him, Kendall looked up at him and licked her lips. "You taste delicious."

"Good lord. I swear you're going to keep me hard as a rock every hour of the day if you keep that up, Kendall."

"Good. We've got a lot of time to make up for." She

smiled as she stood up. "But we do have somewhere to be, don't we?"

"Unfortunately." Kam looked like he didn't want to be anywhere but here. He reached for the bar of soap and started to wash her from tip to toe. Kendall enjoyed the gentle hands that cleansed her body. Her body was still sore and aching with need, but she would make him take care of her later. Probably much later, but it would be worth the wait. That she was sure of.

When she was all clean, she stepped out of the shower and pulled a towel down from the rack over the toilet. She handed one to Kam too. "I've never found a shower to be so... pleasant."

"I'm suddenly a big fan of staying clean. Might have to shower at least three times a day." He winked at her.

"Mmmm...that would be heaven." She reached over and put her hand between his legs. "I can't seem to get enough of you, Kam."

His eyes flashed golden fire. "Neither can I of you, but it will have to be enough for now."

"Right," she sighed. "I can be ready in fifteen."

"Good." He slapped her ass with his hand. "Get on it, woman."

She giggled and slipped out of the room. Even though the shadows were just inches away from her mind, Kam had become the light that Esme had predicted. If she could wrap up the happiness she felt whenever he was around, it would carry her through her darkest times. She was sure of it. She found herself to be a very fortunate woman right now.

CHAPTER 11

As they drove in his car, Kendall was starting to have all kinds of reservations. What if his mother hated her? She didn't even know if his brothers liked her. She'd barely met them. There were so many variables that raced in her head that she was having trouble focusing on staying in the moment. How was she going to get through this? Every inch of her wanted to jump out of the car and race off into the forest. That would be so much easier than facing what she thought would be the end of their relationship because she imagined the worst case scenario.

"Kendall...stop worrying," Kam chastised her.

"How do you know I'm worried?" She held her chin up as she looked out the window.

"I can sense it, Kendall. That's the beauty of being connected. Of course, that also means less privacy at times."

"Oh? How does that work?" Kendall asked him curiously.

Like this. His mouth never moved, but she could hear him as clear as day inside her head. She closed one of her eyes and peered closely at him. How was that possible? And how did she do it? "How did you...?"

"Just focus, Kendall. It will come to you." He smiled at

her.

Focus? That was easier said than done. Her thoughts were all a jumbled mess. Echoes of her past were still just beneath the surface, even though she was trying to shove them deep down inside her. If only she could pretend that none of it had happened. That would make her life a lot easier. Unfortunately, her past would always define her, no matter how much she wanted to pretend it didn't exist.

Are you trying? His words seemed to tease her, but not nearly as much as his grin did.

She crossed her arms over her chest. *Yes!*

There you go! Kam smiled at her and gave her a reassuring nod.

"So whenever I'm overwhelmed by your parents or brothers, I can ask you to rescue me without them knowing?"

"Yes," he chuckled. "But I imagine you'll not need to use it. You're too hard on yourself, Kendall."

"Nasty habit, I guess."

"I plan to break you of that." He promised her.

"Oh? How are you going to do that?" Her thoughts turned back to their morning together, and she wondered if he had more of the same planned for that. She could use some more experience with him. Especially if they picked up right where they'd left off. She had rather enjoyed taking him into her mouth.

"Kendall...," his voice warned her.

"What?" She asked innocently. It wasn't like she put it to words.

"I may not be able to read those thoughts, but I have a pretty good idea where they are headed." His eyes flashed briefly.

"You have a problem with that?" Her eyebrows rose challengingly.

"No, but at the moment we don't have time to explore them." His voice seemed a little gruff.

"What's the matter?" She unbuttoned one of her top buttons so he could see the skin in the valley of her breasts.

"Kendall...."

"I'm a little hot," she offered up. She was hot, burning up just at the thought of what he would do to her next.

"Don't make me turn this car around," he threatened.

"Promise?" That would certainly keep her from having to deal with his family. At least for today. She was fairly certain he would still make her deal with them later, though.

"Chicken," he teased her.

"I am not a chicken."

"Liar." A small chuckle left his mouth.

"Fine. So meeting your family does make me feel a little scared. I mean, it's not like other situations. They're kind of stuck with me, aren't they?"

"That's true."

"Whether they like me or not." Kendall clasped her hands together in her lap, her nervousness translating clearer than any other emotion.

"Relax, Kendall. They'll love you." His words were soft and encouraging as his mind whispered to her, *Just like I do*.

Closing her eyes, she took in a slow breath of air and released it. "I hope so."

She looked at the window again, thinking about her own parents. They would have loved Kam. He represented everything they had ever wanted for her—except for the werewolf part. She probably wouldn't have shared that with them. That would have sent them over the edge in some kind of religious histrionics. Of course, years ago, she would have enjoyed upsetting them. That was when she was so angry at the world around her. Now she was terrified of it. Nothing was finite. Everything always seemed to change before she could get any kind of handle on it. It was almost as if she were on a merry go round that never stopped rotating. The horrors echoed around her non-stop as the memories of her life before reared their ugly heads. There was never any way to keep them at bay.

Thankfully, Kam was not intruding on her thoughts right now. She knew he wanted her to be okay, to not dwell on what happened before, but she had to. If she could figure out what Alistair was up to, then she could help stop him. Maybe for good this time. Kendall had not been strong enough to take him down before. She never believed in herself enough to do so. Today she felt almost renewed, invigorated by the love that Kam had brought into her life. With him at her side, she almost felt like she could do anything. Her limits were sky bound, with no glass ceiling to hold her down. All she had to do was not stay trapped within the fear that had kept her powerless.

"We're here."

"What?" Kendall blinked. She had not been paying attention to the scenery that had changed before her. The ride had not taken nearly as long as she hoped it would. Taking a deep breath, she gave him a weak smile. "You promise they're not going to hate me?"

Kam reached for her hand and brought it to his mouth. "I promise."

Closing her eyes, Kendall tried to still the thoughts that rotated in her head. She needed to just stay in the moment and forget about the darkness that she kept well beneath the surface. She could not afford to let it taint her first meeting with them. Instead, she focused on the beauty that was the man before her. He was her rock, her love, and her life. Kendall would not let him down.

She opened her eyes. "Let's do this."

"That's my girl." Kam squeezed her hand one last time before he let it go.

Kendall unbuckled her seat belt and opened the car door. She'd barely gotten out of the car before two little girls came racing over to her. The younger one grabbed her hands and tugged on her.

"Are you our auntie now?" the younger one asked her.

"Uh...." She looked over to Kam helplessly.

He grinned at her. "Don't look at me. That's all you."

"Thanks," she grumbled.

"Don't be rude, Sophie." The older girl shook her head at her cousin. "I'm Taela."

"And I'm Sophie!" The girl exclaimed with so much charm; it was hard to not let it warm her heart.

"Hello, Sophie and Taela." She smiled at them. "I bet you keep your uncle on his toes."

Kam chuckled. "Definitely."

"Are you our auntie now?" Sophie asked again.

Kendall knelt down and looked into the little girl's eyes. How could she resist such charm? "Would you like that?"

"Yes!" Sophie jumped up and down.

A tear started to form in her eye, and she squeezed her eyes shut for a second. "I would like that, Sophie."

"Good. She wasn't going to stop until you said yes," giggled Taela.

"Perseverance is a lovely trait. Always stick to your guns." Kendall winked at Sophie before offering her hand to Taela too. "I don't suppose you'd like to show me around, would you?"

"Of course! You'll want to meet my brothers too." Taela grabbed her hand.

"Why? All they do is drool and poop." Sophie wrinkled her nose.

"Are you sisters too?" asked Kendall.

"I wish!" exclaimed Taela. "Sophie's my cousin. She has a little sister named Emily. My brothers are Kristian and Keegan."

"I see. Well, lead the way."

Apparently, Kam's entire family was there. She was starting to think that she should have stayed at home. Then again, the girls were so sweet to her; it was hard to deny them. She had a feeling she would spend a fair amount of time spoiling them rotten if she were given the chance.

"I'll leave you to it then." Kam nodded to her.

You're leaving me with them? Kendall almost felt like panicking. What was she going to do with a bunch of kids? What if they led her directly into the wolves' den? That was what this place was, right? The entire pack could be there ready to...what? Tear her down? Last night they had not said much to her. They had given Kam a fair amount of grief.

She had felt protective of him. That was probably par for the course. She knew in her heart that she would protect him at all costs.

You're a natural. His voice seemed to be teasing her, and she made a mental note to get him back for it later. She did not feel like a natural at all. She was way out of her league where children were concerned. The last child she had dealt with...well, that was when she was a child herself. Kendall had absolutely no experience with them at all. It wasn't like she had thought they would be in her future.

The girls led her into the backyard, where there were children crawling all over the ground. Kendall saw the two women who were watching them and almost panicked. How was she going to introduce herself to them? Shouldn't Kam be doing this? She reminded herself to kill him later, especially if this all went south real fast.

"Mama!" Sophie called to her mother.

"Yes, ladybug?" Brina looked up and smiled. "Well, you must be Kendall."

"Uh, yeah." Kendall already felt like she was going to trip all over her words.

"Relax. We've all felt the way you do right now," she assured her. "I'm Brina. You've already met my daughter, Sophie."

"Mama, she's our auntie now," exclaimed the girl.

"So it seems. Come, sit." Brina gestured to the blankets on the ground.

"You can help us make sure the babies don't start eating grass. I'm Lila." Lila put a hand to her stomach and let out a deep breath. "I swear, the heartburn is even worse the second time around."

"You might be having a girl then. It was rough for me, too, but definitely worth it." Brina's eyes moved to the child who was toddling on the ground. The little girl toppled over and giggled.

"I still can't believe we're already on round two." Lila sighed.

"I have to beat Killian off with a stick most days. These men seem to be extra potent if you ask me," Brina giggled.

If only, Kendall thought to herself. She'd give anything to have the life these two had. Beautiful children, adoring mates, and what looked like bliss. Was it possible for her to have all those things? And would either one of them feel as fulfilled if Kendall were unable to give Kam the children he deserved?

"Round two?" Kendall asked curiously as she looked at the oldest child.

"We adopted Taela," explained Lila.

"Oh." So adoption didn't seem to put a damper on the Knight clan. Would that be enough for Kam, though? She shook her head and tried to keep her morose thoughts at bay. "You all have such lovely children."

Brina snorted. "For now. Wait until the witching hour."

"Witching hour?" Kendall wondered what she meant by that.

"In probably twenty minutes, one of the twins is going to start crying. That will make the other one start. And then Emily will cry just to not be left out," Lila explained.

"It's like clockwork these days. You kind of get used to it." Brina sighed and held out a pacifier to one of the boys who had crawled over to her.

"Well, at least we have an extra set of hands." Lila nodded to Kendall.

"Oh, I don't know about that. I don't have much experience with children." Kendall was suddenly terrified of staying here with the women. Had she known it would make her a volunteer babysitter, she would have followed Kam into the house and dealt with meeting his mother for the first time.

"You'll get plenty soon enough." Lila nodded to her belly.

"Oh, I don't know about that. I mean...it's probably not even something...." Kendall coughed and sputtered slightly.

"You just never know," Lila continued. "Knight men often have fertile women."

Kendall looked down at the ground. "And what if they're not?"

"It wouldn't change a thing," Brina assured her.

"Will his mother—?"

"She'll love you because Kam does. We've all worried about him for far too long." Brina put a hand on hers. "You can stop worrying. Amber was thrilled to hear he had taken a mate. You could be Medusa, and she'd throw her arms around you."

"Well," Kendall touched her hair and bit the bottom of her lip. "I may not be ugly enough to turn someone to stone, but I do have my faults."

"We all do. Well look, here comes Amber now." Lila nodded to Kam, who was walking his mother out of the house.

"Crap," she uttered under her breath.

"She doesn't bite much anymore," Brina teased her.

Kendall felt mortified. "Best to get this over with, I guess."

Kendall was about to rise to her feet when Emily toppled

into her lap, giggling. Kendall smiled at her and helped to right her. The child would not leave her, though. Instead, she wrapped her arms around her neck and kissed her on the cheek. Kendall wrapped her arms around her and hugged the little girl tight. Unable to get up, she stayed where she was and listened to the little girl chatter at her as she pointed to the sky.

"Yes, love. I see. The sky. Was there a bird?"

"Bir....bir...." Emily's big blue eyes were wide open as she touched her fingers to Kendall's mouth.

"Yes, bird." Kendall pointed to the nearest tree. "They like to sit in trees when they're not flying."

"Oooohhh fly!" Emily opened her arms up wide.

"Eh hem. Allow me." Kam scooped the girl up in his arms and tossed her up into the air. The world was filled with high pitched squeals as Kam continued to make her fly.

Kendall felt tears spring to her eyes and tried to shut them out. She turned to find Amber Knight watching her thoughtfully. Kendall sprung to her feet. "Hello. I'm Kendall, and you are—"

"Amber. Care to take a walk?" She offered her arm to Kendall.

Kendall took the arm under the encouraging stares of the women before her. Her thoughts raced inside her, so randomly that she could barely hold on to them. She had to literally remind herself to keep them shut out of her brain.

"You're worried." Amber interrupted her mad mental cycle.

"Yes," Kendall admitted.

"About what?" Amber asked her.

"That I'll never be good enough," Kendall almost whispered.

"Oh, child. You are more than good enough. You are absolutely perfect for him."

Kendall looked up at her in surprise. "I don't understand."

"I don't suppose you do. I've always known that Kam was pining for something. I never quite understood it. But I do now. You both were waiting for each other, after all." Amber patted her hand. "No matter what came before, it is what you do in the here, and now that makes all the difference."

"Do you really think so?" This time Kendall knew the tears were going to fall before she could stop them.

"I do. You look like you could use a hug, dear." Amber held her arms open.

Kendall faltered for just a moment before she let Amber hold her tight. The calm, soothing energy that enveloped her almost took her breath away. She sighed against her as Kendall laid her head on her shoulder. It was almost as if she had her mother back with her, the one who had loved her so fiercely long ago. Kendall couldn't remember the last time she had hugged her mother. Even when she was sick, the connection had been lost. She was sorry for that. Her mother had probably needed more than Kendall had been willing to give. It wasn't that she didn't want to love people. She was just so tired of disappointing them.

"She loved you, you know." Amber ran her hand over Kendall's back. "But she knew you wouldn't believe her. Not with the dark mark over your heart."

Kendall moved away from her and held her hand up. "What are you talking about?"

"The one that the dark caster placed over you. You've been fighting it ever since, yes?"

"Alistair." Kendall looked down at the ground.

"Not to worry, Kendall. We shall erase his narrative from your life. That is a guarantee." Amber's body was rigid as if she were preparing for a fight.

"I should not have brought this into your family."

"Bah! He's one man. We've taken down thousands, living and dead. He doesn't scare any of us."

"Don't underestimate Alistair. He is quite powerful. It will be hard to find his weakness."

"Ah, but we already know his weakness, dear."

"Which is?" Kendall couldn't imagine Alistair had a weak bone in his body.

"You."

"What?" Kendall gasped. She had to be kidding. There was no way Alistair held her in any light, except as that of a possession. More than anything, he was furious that he had lost her. Nothing more.

"We'll get that sorted later, my dear. Right now, Kam is worried we might not be getting along." Amber nodded to where Kam stood by a tree.

Kendall snorted. "And he told me I had nothing to worry about."

"I may have made him think I was going to toss him out on his ass for not telling us about you sooner." Amber grinned at her.

"You wouldn't."

"No, but he doesn't know that. Now, let's get the party started, shall we?"

"Party?" Kendall wondered what they were celebrating.

"Yes, it's a welcome to the family party. The boys have promised to be on their best behavior. You've met all of them, except Kendrick, who is away on a dig right now."

"A dig?"

"Oh yes, big into anthropology and archaeology, apparently. I still think he's chasing a skirt there, but that's just me. Anyway, I'll head inside so you can assure him that you have come to no harm." Amber smiled in amusement.

Kendall watched Amber Knight walk away and waited for Kam to walk over to her. She met him halfway and smiled up at him. "You have a wonderful family."

"They're yours now too." His thumb ran across her cheek.

Kendall put her head on his chest and breathed a sigh of relief. She had been really worried that they would not accept her. Her past made her feel unworthy of him. It was hard to shake that feeling. Kendall knew she had a long way to go where that was concerned. With Kam at her side, she almost felt like she could take on the world.

CHAPTER 12

When they went into the house, Kendall was surrounded by loud, blustery males, all vying for her attention. She had no idea what she was supposed to do with so many men surrounding her. "One at a time?"

"How in the hell did you manage to land this one?" Kyle shook his head at Kam. "I mean, if it were me, I could see—"

Kendall shook her head at Kyle. "You're quite the prick, aren't you?"

A chorus of loud laughs echoed around her. Kam just stood there with his arms crossed over his chest, beaming at her. Kyle had the decency to look down at the ground and mumbled something about it takes one to know one. His cheeks were red.

"I think she's a gem," laughed Kenton Knight.

"I think so too." Kam wrapped his arm around her shoulders comfortingly.

Kendall was still trying to figure out how she felt about being accepted into such a large family. Having only a few distant relatives, their get togethers had never been nearly as loud and unruly as this one. Kendall wondered if they were always like this. She smiled and looked around the room. The

Knights were clearly a blessed family.

Kendall knew she and Kam were a new couple, but she hoped that they endured over time. She had never asked for the specifics of the arrangement. All she knew was when a werewolf claimed its mate, that was the person they would spend the rest of his life with. Or hers. There were probably a fair share of women werewolves too. She wasn't exactly sure, for Kam was the only one she had met up until this point. Unless she included the Knight men standing before her.

"We had actually almost given up hope for him," teased Karter.

"You're one to talk," Kam almost growled.

"Hey, don't hate the player, hate the game." Karter's smile was bright until Lila walked into the room.

"Game my ass. It's your time to change the boys, by the way." She had one boy on each hip.

"Right."

Kendall was reminded of a puppy who was heading back to his master. It was clear that Lila ruled that roost. It actually appeared as if the women had a fair amount of power in their relationships. That was definitely something Kendall could get behind. She wondered how Kam would react to that. He didn't seem to be as macho as some of his other brothers. Or was that just the way he acted around her?

Karter turned to see Kam making a face at him. "Hey, just you wait until it's your turn to do the doody."

The room broke into another round of laughter. Kendall was the only one who didn't laugh. They all expected him to have the same thing they did. Kendall wasn't even sure that was possible. She nibbled her bottom lip and took a slow breath in. Right now, she needed to not focus on that. Even if she were able to have children, there was a monster out there who would continue to haunt her until she put an end to his power. The binding spell she had cast only seemed to work for short periods of time. When was the last time she had cast it? Six months ago? It was a spell she seemed to have on repeat. Whenever she felt him growing nearer to her again, she would do another ritual to protect herself. It was getting downright annoying now.

As if sensing her angst, Kam kissed her on top of the head. She blushed as several pairs of eyes saw his display of affection. Kendall had never really been in this situation before. She was slightly uncomfortable. Maybe it was because the last man she had been close to had held his affections aside like some kind of mental warfare strategy. She shivered slightly and tried to push the darkness away.

"Let's eat." Amber gestured to the dining room.

Kendall followed the others to the table and was surprised at the feast that had been put together. It reminded her of a Thanksgiving dinner. That was a lot of food. She sat down and put her napkin in her lap, wondering what kind of table manners were acceptable in this situation. Before long, it became very clear that the Knights did not need pomp and circumstance. They started to scoop food onto their plates amidst even more talking. Kendall smiled brightly at the mad chaos around her. His family was definitely nothing like she expected, and yet they were perfect.

"We're not so scary, are we?" asked Killian from across the table.

"No...I suppose not." She picked up a chicken leg and

put it on her plate. Kendall could not remember the last time she had fried chicken. It smelled delicious. She added some mashed potatoes and corn on the cob. Before she knew it, her plate looked like a small avalanche of food. She couldn't help it, though. All of it smelled so good.

Eat up. You're going to need your strength.

Kendall almost dropped her fork at his words. What was he planning? She turned to glance at him and saw he had a mischievous look on his face. She pursed her lips and shook her head. Taking a bite of her food, she felt his hand slide onto her lap. Clearly, he was feeling randy, especially since his eyes were flashing every few seconds. Kendall looked around the table to see if anyone else noticed. Thankfully, they were all engrossed with their food.

You're playing with fire. She scrunched her nose and licked some of the mashed potatoes off her fingertip. Kendall was rewarded with another flash of golden light as his fingers dug into her leg. He released her and went back to his food. She may have won this round with him, but she had a feeling she would pay for it later. All kinds of wicked thoughts raced through her head.

Thankfully, the feast was uneventful. It wasn't until the children were sorted and asleep that the adults really started to get down to business. Kendall knew something was up. She sat down on the couch and waited to see what they were about to talk about.

"Kendall, Kam has been telling us about Alistair." Amber started the conversation off.

"Yes." Kendall fought the urge to look down at the floor. She was embarrassed about her past. "He's not a good man

116

at all."

"Dark caster?" asked Kenton.

"Of the worst sort. He feeds off innocent witches, taking their light one day at a time. I was lucky to escape." Kendall did not know how else to describe it.

"That would explain some of the missing girls," Killian said thoughtfully.

"We were afraid they were dead," Amber explained.

"Not yet. But if he has his way, it won't be long. Only the strongest were able to survive his grip over them."

Kendall had never thought about herself as strong until this moment. It was true, though. Many girls had come and gone in the dungeon. They had not been able to fight off the darkness that Alistair wove around them. That, or he could not get his clutches on their powers. She had often felt guilty for surviving for so long. Part of her wondered if any of the others had figured out how she escaped.

Looking back, even now, she wasn't entirely sure how she had managed. Kendall had made herself as small as possible, locking her magic deep inside her to conserve it. She had started to starve herself, making it look as if she were dying. Her act had been convincing enough to make him cast her to the side for a bit. When he stopped paying attention to her, she started to manifest her magic in new ways—telekinesis, something that wasn't a common occurrence in the witch world. She had used her mind to steal the key to her cage. Kendall was actually lucky that no one had seen the object flying through the air. That was the one time she was glad that his dungeon had been so dark.

"So, how do we stop him?" asked Kam.

"Bait," Kendall answered.

"Excuse me?" Kam clamped his mouth shut. "Absolutely not."

"I agree. That's risky." Killian shook his head. "There has to be another way."

Kendall sighed. She knew there was no other way, but she was sure that Kam would not see reason on that. To go against him would probably put quite a strain on their relationship, so Kendall would not go behind his back. Not unless she had no other choice.

"You have to find his dungeon. Cut off his supply. He grows strong off draining magic from witches."

"How can we track him?" Amber asked her.

"My guess is keeping an eye around the witch camp?" Brina suggested.

If only that would really work, Kendall wanted to say. Right now, though, she couldn't voice those concerns. No one really knew anything about Alistair. Not like she did. He would not stop until he had drained every drop of life from those around him. If he were teaching new dark casters, how to do this, the balance of the world would certainly be in trouble. She wasn't even sure her input would be accepted at this point. Kam seemed determined to shut her out of it.

"What is his usual victim?" Karter asked her.

"Young, lost, alone, innocent," Kendall answered almost tonelessly.

She had been all those things. Right now, the only thing she didn't feel was innocent. The sins she had committed reared their ugly head at her. How many times had Alistair made her take part in his torture? She had not been a willing participant, but the girls all had an understanding. It was better to give than to take. Any one of them would have done the same. Some of them actually enjoyed it. They were being molded into dark casters themselves. Alistair prided himself on corrupting light workers. It was one of his favorite things. She shivered when she remembered how close Ilah had been to being just that when Kendall had broken free. Had she outlived her usefulness? That, or was she becoming too powerful for him to manipulate?

"We're going to find him," promised Amber.

Kendall smiled at the woman. "Yes, I believe we will."

"And then we'll put an end to that asshole." Kam slammed his fist into his hand, and Kendall almost jumped out of her skin.

"Did he forget to tell you about his nasty temper?" Karter asked her.

"Temper?" Kendall looked over at Kam. She saw her mate wanting to protect her. He was no threat to her — to her assailant, perhaps. Kendall had no problem visualizing him ripping a man's throat out if they deserved it. He'd probably had all the military training for that. And if the human couldn't do it, the wolf could do it with very little effort. Kendall was lucky to have both of them on her side.

"Let's just say we've all had our moments with him." Killian grinned.

"You usually deserved it too," Kam grumbled.

"Hmph. You say that now." Kyle rolled his eyes.

"I take it you've gotten stomped the most?" Kendall rolled her eyes.

"No...." Kyle was now pouting.

"She's got your number for sure," Karter chuckled loudly.

"Yeah? Just wait until Kendrick comes home. Then you can start picking on him again."

Kendall snorted. "If he's anything like you, we'll have our hands full."

"Have I told you how much I like her?" Killian was grinning from ear to ear.

"Feisty," Karter agreed.

"We need more strong women to keep these guys in line," Brina added.

"Hey, I've been good." Killian held his hands up in protest.

"In a pig's eye," snorted Brina.

Kendall sighed and shook her head at the chaos around her. It was simply beautiful. She wondered if Kam knew how lucky he was to have all of them. As more time passed, the group started to shuffle out the door. They had children to put to bed in their own homes, after all. What she wouldn't give for that dilemma. That was a problem for another day, though. Today, she was more focused on how she could help the Knights find Alistair and take him out. She had not promised not to take action, but she would watch her step for now.

CHAPTER 13

When they finally made their way back home, Kendall was still stuck in her thoughts. She had trouble climbing out of them. That was understandable, considering all the ways her mind was turning. Being accepted into a family was great, but it still didn't help her understand her place. Was she just there to mate with him? In a normal situation, they would have dated for a while and then made the next step. It seemed to her that several steps had been skipped along the way. As sad as it was to think of, it was probably better that her mother wasn't around to see the mess in her life right now. Her mother would want her married.

Was marriage important, though? Not really. Kendall did not need a piece of paper to know that Kam was devoted to her. She could feel it any time she was around him. It carried her through the times when he wasn't, too. The moment he had claimed her, her life had changed. She was still trying to figure out what to do with those changes. They were living in a cabin that he had sold her.

"I'm curious," Kendall started to ask.

"About?"

"What is it that you do when you're not...?" She waved

a hand from his head to toe. "Doing what you do with your pack?"

"I'm a property manager for Knight Properties. The cabin I sold you was one of many of ours."

"I thought you said you were in between houses?"

"I was living there while my house was being finished." Kam's eyes twinkled.

"You're building a house?" Kendall asked in disbelief.

"My family is wealthy enough that I do not have to actually work, Kendall. I choose to manage the properties. I take care of the tenants, collect the rent, fix any property issues. I like to be useful."

"I was cleaning houses until my mom died. I'm still trying to figure out what I do next." Kendall clenched her hands together as her thoughts seemed to rotate in her head. What was the next step for her? How long could she be content to sit around and do nothing?

"You have time to figure it out. Mind if we take a detour?" Kam asked her. He had a smile on his face that she couldn't quite read.

"Sure." Kendall wondered what he was up to. Where were they headed?

The car turned down Wash Avenue and followed the road until there was nothing but trees all around them. The gravel popped under the tires as Kam pulled down a gravel road. When they made their way down the long drive, Kendall saw a two-story house that looked like something out of a fairy tale.

"Care to take a look?"

"Are you kidding me?"

The car had barely stopped before Kendall hopped out the door. The brick house with its arched entryway was stunning. She could see into it through the tall windows that she imagined let in enough sunlight to light the entire house. She wondered what the house looked like on the inside, and whether Kam was going to show her through it.

She turned to him with a bright smile on her face. "This is beautiful."

"It's ours." He had the air of a man who was proud of his accomplishments.

"Ours?" Kendall felt like her jaw must have dropped to the ground.

"I told you, I don't have to worry about money. We are well provided for, Kendall."

"You are," she reminded him. Kendall wasn't sure how much she fit into his world. She did not make assumptions. Nothing in life was a guarantee.

Kam pulled her into his arms and forced her to look in his eyes. "Mates are for life, Kendall. I'll not have another. What's mine is yours."

She was startled at his words. "But—"

"No buts. My family knows my choice. If something were to happen to me, they would make sure you were well taken care of."

"Why?" She had nothing to give them in return, and it wasn't like she could guarantee further growth of their family tree.

"Because I love you, Kendall. Come, I have a story to share with you." Kam unlocked the door and opened it wide.

Kendall followed him inside, curious as to what his story

would include. When she entered the house, she almost gasped in delight. The floors were a dark cherry wood that matched the wood on the staircase. She could see the moonlight streaming onto the floor below. The whole house was a blank canvas, with stark white walls that were screaming for someone to come in and put the right touch to them.

Kam led her into the large family room and turned to look out the window. "Kyle, he's the only one that knew this."

"Knew what?"

Kam pulled the photo out of his wallet and held it up to her. "This photo doesn't represent Hannah to me."

"It doesn't?" She asked in confusion.

"Do you see the crease?" His finger pointed down the center.

"Yeah?"

"I folded it over a long time ago because my wolf knew what I was ashamed to admit."

Kendall was having trouble following his words. What exactly did he mean? What was he ashamed of?

"There I was, miles away from home, pining for someone who was not much more than a child."

"Me?" Kendall almost squeaked. "You're telling me, all the time I was fantasizing about you, you were—"

"Having wet dreams about a sweet teenage girl? Yes...it was embarrassing." He grinned at her.

"Were they good ones?" She asked him. Kendall was almost curious as to what he had imagined they would do. Maybe they could make up for some lost time and try a few of those scenarios out. She'd had a limited imagination herself. Kam had already exceeded her wildest dreams. Surely there was a lot more to explore.

Kam almost choked with laughter. "Here I was worried that would upset you."

"No, not at all. It kind of makes sense."

"How so?" Kam asked her.

"Well, you see, if you are supposed to have one mate you are destined to be with, seeing them would put them on your radar, right?" That might be why she had such a hard time when she was younger too. While she had gone out and had a relationship with Alistair, clearly, that was not meant to work. She wondered how many women he had known. "Can I ask you a question?"

"Anything."

"How many women have you had a relationship with?"

Kam seemed a little ruffled by her question. "I'm not a saint. I've had a few one night stands, some hook-ups here and there. Nothing seemed to stick, though."

Kendall sensed his nervousness. She put her hand on his arm. "Good."

"Good?" He looked at her as if she had a high fever or some kind of delirium.

"Yes. Because when you say there's only me, I know you've had other choices. I know that doesn't make a lot of sense, but if I were your one and only, I would wonder if I was enough eventually."

"And you, Kendall?"

"Besides my time with Alistair, there's only been you." She sighed. "I wish there had only been you."

"It's not your fault, Kendall." Kam pulled her into his arms and stroked the back of her hair. "Some men are predators.

They prey on the innocent, chew them up, and spit them out. You were lucky to come out on the other side."

"I was weak." Kendall refused to allow herself to take the easy way out.

"You were lonely and lost." Kam kissed her forehead. "Stop being so hard on yourself. Whether you ever met Alistair or not, he would still be doing what he did. Having an outsider that lived to tell the story is a weapon that can take him down."

"Do you really think so?" Kendall wanted to help, however she could. She was afraid that Kam would prevent her from doing what she needed to in the end, though. There was no way he would let her out to find him. He was protective — that, anyone could tell.

"We will bring that asshole down, mark my words." His voice was gruff as if anger was just beneath the surface. "But, let's not talk about that tonight. Instead, I have a surprise for you."

"A surprise?" Kendall pushed away from him. "I'm not sure I can handle many more surprises. A house...what's next, Kam?"

"This." Kam pulled something out of his pocket and knelt down on the floor before her. "You have been my light for longer than you know, Kendall. You are everything I have ever wanted in a mate and a wife. I would be the happiest man alive if you would make me an honest man."

"You, honest?" Kendall burst out laughing, more in nervousness than anything else.

"Is that a yes?" His eyebrow rose curiously.

"Yes, Kameron Knight, I will marry you, just so you are

stuck with my annoying ass for the rest of your life," she teased him as he slid the ring over her finger.

"I hope you like it." Kam nodded to the ring.

The simple rose quartz gemstone surrounded by a circle of diamonds was so beautiful that tears started to pool in her eyes. "It's beautiful, Kam! When did you have time to find this?"

"When I left, I did a lot of soul searching. Trying to find out how to be the man you deserved. It led me to many different places, including every jewelry store I could find. I wanted something that reminded me of the gentle nature you keep hidden beneath. You're often hard when you want to be soft."

How did he know that? His words were absolutely spot on. Even when she was rebelling as a teen, she had felt like a lost child that just wanted to be comforted by someone who cared. Her parents were so worried about her heading down the wrong path that they had not invested time in getting to know what it was that she needed. Had they understood that school was too hard for her, they may not have pushed for her to give up the only thing she cared about. It wasn't that Kendall was not book smart. She just had trouble keeping all that information in her head, especially math and science. Those two subjects had always been her hardest. Rather than punish her for her shortcomings, they could have found another way to approach it. Kendall promised herself that if she were able to have children in any way, she would try to be more understanding than her own parents had been. She would also make sure that they all knew how important they were, and that not one child was more important than the other.

"This is beautiful, Kam. You are everything I've ever wanted, and so much more."

"Does the reality measure up to the dream?" He asked her softly.

"Reality is so much better." She nuzzled her head against his shoulder. His arms came around her and held her tightly against him. The moment would only have been better if she did not have a darkness hanging over them. She didn't want to think about the immediate future. If she could just forget Alistair existed, her life would be complete.

"Do you want a tour? Killian designed it for me. While his company built it, we all pitched in some time here and there. I think you're going to like the back the most."

"Oh?" Kendall was now very curious. "Lead the way, then."

Kam led her into the kitchen, and Kendall almost lost her mind. It was the largest kitchen she had ever seen. The marble countertops seemed to go on forever. There was a cooktop and a double convection oven. Kendall couldn't wait to cook up a feast here. If she learned how that was. It couldn't be that hard, right? This was the first time she had stepped into a kitchen that made her want to learn how to make something irresistible. "This is huge."

"Well, we often take turns hosting the meals, so we needed enough space to get it all done."

"I like your family." Kendall ran a hand along the marble counter. "They seem so nice. Well, most of them. That Kyle... he needs an adjustment."

Kam burst out laughing. "Oh, yes, you are definitely going to fit in. It used to be Karter that got the most grief.

Now Kyle's the front runner, it seems."

"I'm guessing he earned that title, though," Kendall told herself to behave.

"So, you'll need to help with color schemes, Kendall. Whatever you want, we'll get it done."

"But this is our house, Kam. We should make those decisions together." She shook a finger at him. "Don't think you're getting out of making decisions, sir."

"Damn...you got me." He winked at her. "I'm not a fan of dark colors."

"Me either. What about beach colors? They're light and airy, some pastel, some earth tones."

"Sounds nice. We'll have to get some samples. Come with me."

Kendall tilted her head at him, wondering what he was up to now. She followed him outside and almost squealed in delight. "You've got a pool?"

"We've got a pool, and it's heated, so even when it's colder outside, we can use it. See the far end there?" Kam pointed to the back where there was a smaller pool.

"Yes?"

"Hot tub." He grinned at her.

"So, you've got the pool all set up. What's missing from this house?" Kendall wondered why he thought it wasn't ready yet.

"Final light features, paint, and finishing the rest of the basement. Do you want to see the rest?"

"Are you kidding me?" Kendall rolled her eyes at him and left him standing there by the water's edge. She walked into the house and headed upstairs. There was a total of four bedrooms, including the largest master bedroom she had ever seen in her life. That room could fit almost her entire cabin in it. There was certainly no shortage of space. The master bath was pretty impressive too. Kendall was starting to feel like she had walked into some kind of fantasy world. It wasn't like her family home had been small, it was just that this was such a change from what she was used to. She was starting to feel like she had moved up in the world.

Kam's voice interrupted her thoughts. "Too much?"

She turned to face him with a bright smile on her face. "It's amazing, Kam. I never imagined a life this wonderful.'

"Only the best for my mate," Kam smiled. "Besides, it barely makes up for my shortcomings. I'm incredibly grumpy without my morning coffee."

"Who isn't?" She gave him a half-smile. "I love you no matter what faults you think you're hiding from me."

"You have a lot of work to do."

"Oh? What kind of work?"

"You're in charge of decorating our den." His grin was huge.

"Chicken," she teased him.

"I'll show you who's chicken." He stepped toward her, and she backed up.

"What are you doing?" She held a hand up.

"Why, are you afraid?" he asked her when his hands reached behind her back.

"No," she whispered against his mouth just before it touched hers.

Kam backed her up against the wall. His mouth distracted her as his hands slid up her shirt. His hands were warm on her skin, and she trembled beneath him. His thumb made small circles around her nipple, and she sighed against him.

When he pushed her shirt up and over her head, Kendall eyed him warily. "Kam...you do realize there's no bed in here, right?"

"We'll improvise." He unhooked her bra and kissed her shoulders before sliding the straps slowly down.

She shivered in anticipation when he slid down her body. He knelt before her and brought one of her breasts to his mouth. He teased it with his tongue as he sucked her into his mouth. Kendall arched into him as a delicious fire started to flow through her veins. He could do whatever he wanted to her, but if she ended up with rug burns, she would tell him a thing or two. When he removed her bottoms, she saw a fire light his eyes. He was filled with a need that only she could quench. Knowing that only made her more excited.

When Kam's scruff brushed against the inside of her legs, she shivered in anticipation. He spread her legs and started to devour her core. His tongue slid against her clit, and she moaned so loud, it almost echoed in the room around them. He nibbled on her and sucked her into his mouth just as he stuck his finger inside her. Kendall thought she was going to lose her mind. The fever rushing inside her was rising as he brought her to the brink with very little effort.

He growled against her as he lapped up her juices. "So sweet...."

Kendall put her hands on his shoulders to steady herself as he continued to work his magic over her. By the time he finally stood up, Kendall's legs felt like jelly.

Kam had a grin on his face. "How you doing?"

"As if you didn't know." Her eyelids felt heavy and sensual as desire coursed through her entire body. She tugged at his pants, her need to feel him deep inside her overpowering every other thought in her head.

Kam took her cue and removed his clothing. When he was done, he picked her up off the ground and moved her back against the wall. He slid his cock inside her and started to pump into her. Kendall wrapped her legs around him and held on for the ride. She was not disappointed in the slightest. Kam was a strong lover, able to hold her up and take her over the edge almost effortlessly. The fire that burned between them was so hot, she wondered how they had not set the house on fire.

"That's right, Kendall...come on."

His encouragement pushed her over the edge. She trembled around him, and her legs pulled him deeper inside her. Kam was not far behind her. He pushed into her a few more times before he came inside her. "God, yes!"

Kendall closed her eyes and smiled to herself. This was not the life she had ever hoped for. It was so much more than she could ever have imagined. It was almost the happily ever after that every girl dreamed of. If there wasn't a shadow following them around, her life would be perfect. She laid her head on his shoulder and pushed out the dark thoughts. She refused to let them ruin the here and now.

"I love you, Kam," she murmured softly.

"Good. Cause you're stuck with me for better or worse."

"I'm not sure how it could get much better," she sighed against him.

"The sky's the limit, Kendall," he promised her. Kendall

would give anything to believe him.

CHAPTER 14

When they returned to the cabin, Kendall was ready to climb into bed. It had been a long day—a good one, but a long one for sure. When she put on her nightclothes, she was surprised to find that Kam had not followed her into the room. She went to the small living room and found him staring at his phone.

"Something wrong?"

"Yes and no."

"What is it?" Kendall felt like her heart was dropping to the bottom of her feet as she waited for him to answer her.

"Nothing has happened. We've taken shifts to protect the hollow, and it's my turn."

"Oh. Okay. Do you want me to come with you?" Kendall asked him. She was sure she could do something to help. Then again, she might be more of a distraction if she went with him.

"No. I want you to stay here where I know you're safe."

Kendall tried not to take his response personally. She would feel the same way if she were in his shoes. That didn't mean she had to completely behave herself all the time. He was not going to stop her from tracking down Alistair. She'd just have to do it on the down low. If he knew she was trying to find Alistair, Kam would probably lock her in the cabin and sick one of his brothers on her. She did not want that to happen. She barely knew them, and while they seemed to accept her with very few questions, she was still sure they had their concerns. She certainly would not blame them if they did.

Kendall walked over to the couch and kissed him on the cheek. "Be careful, Kam."

"I will." He flashed a grin at her.

"Don't get cocky. No one is invincible. Not even werewolves," she reminded him.

"Noted." Kam kissed her slowly, then let out a slow breath. "Lock the door behind me, Kendall."

"Yes, sir!" She saluted him and saw him smirk at her. "What?"

"Just had a few ideas flash through my head." He grinned.

"Oh?"

"I think I have my uniform somewhere still...."

"That could be trouble." Had she just said that aloud? Kendall looked away from him and blushed.

"I see. Yes, we'll have to find that later." He walked to the door and looked back at her one last time. "Get some rest, Kendall."

"I will." She walked over to the door and ushered him out of it and slapped him on the ass with her hand as he was exiting. "Hurry up, so you can come back to me."

"Yes, ma'am."

Kendall closed the door behind him and locked it. Part of her was tempted to follow right behind him, but she knew he would sense her trailing him. That would put a damper on the rest of the night for sure. Besides, she was still very exhausted. It was as if the past few months had finally caught up to her. The sorrow she had kept hidden far beneath the surface had started to evaporate. It was a slow process and a draining one. Kendall wasn't sure when it would end, either. There was a lifetime of emptiness to replace with new memories, new love. She knew that would take time. Anything worth fighting for did.

Making her way over to the coffee table, she pulled one of the drawers out and started to make an altar on the table before her. Tonight would be a good night for meditation. It would help her reflect on her day while helping her plan for the future. If she were lucky, one of her guides would visit her with some insight as to what direction she needed to head in next. Kendall needed advice from the cosmos. There were things that no one else could show her.

Lighting the candles, she said a silent prayer to each direction, asking for protection as she cast a small circle around herself. Closing her eyes, she imagined the white ball of light at her core. It grew slowly until it surrounded every inch of her space. When she felt the gentle ebb and flow of energy around her, she opened her eyes.

Whenever she meditated, it was almost as if she were in a different universe altogether. Gone was the cabin floor. It had been replaced with an earthen floor. The walls were no longer there. Instead, she was surrounded by tall evergreen trees. A small breeze blew against her face as she breathed in the fresh air around her. Small pink symbols floated in the air around her face, and she touched one at a time. Time and change were the first two she understood. She had entered the circle wanting to know where her life should be headed. The universe had heard her questions.

The next symbol she touched was joy. Kendall knew that Kam brought a lot of joy into her life, but she had a feeling this was not in regards to what he had done for her, but something she would have to retrieve herself. It was almost as if they were telling her to find her joy again. What was her joy outside of Kam? It was something that had been missing in her life for quite some time. An image of a pirouette danced across her mind, and Kendall knew what it was that was missing. Dance. How was she going to bring dance back into her life? She was far too old to start over. A career would have happened a long time ago for her if she had been destined to walk that path.

She thought about it a little harder and realized that the only thing holding her back at this point was herself. It would only be a disservice to herself if she didn't at least look into some avenue that would lead her back to dance. Maybe she could take a few adult classes? Or teach a class to little ones? That could be fun, perhaps. She'd have to take a look at her options to see where they might lead her.

As Kendall started to look at the next symbol before her, she read caution. Great, so her guides wanted her to follow her dreams, yet wanted her to be cautious. How could one follow a dream that was always just out of reach because she was afraid to go after it? Maybe the caution wasn't related to that at all. Kendall pursed her lips thoughtfully and willed the next word to show up.

Darkness. She shivered. So the caution was not for

following the next path in her life but reflecting on the shadows of her past that never seemed too far away. Curling her fingers into her legs, she took a deep breath and tried to remain calm. She almost sensed him reaching out for her. Kendall would have to be careful. As much as she wanted to catch him, she did not want him to ruin everything she had going for her right now.

Part of her wondered what would have happened had she never met Alistair. Would she be sitting here, happily engaged to the sexiest man on earth? Would she have found him earlier? That was entirely possible. However, she knew that while she didn't like to believe it, sometimes things happened for a reason. Even death had a purpose. Everyone had time here on earth, and some lives were more limited than others. Like her sister. Kendall missed her dearly, but her sacrifice had saved several lives, and that was worth remembering.

Kendall sighed. She wished she could talk to Hannah. Part of her was worried that her sister would be upset with the way things had turned out. Kendall had known how much Hannah cared for Kam. If she were alive, Kendall would never have let herself fall for him the way she had. Instead, she would have carried her crush to the grave and probably been miserable for the rest of her life. Kendall smiled as she thought about the younger Kam fantasizing about a sixteen-year-old girl. She stifled a giggle. The idea was almost absurd, and yet she believed him. Kam had no reason to lie about it.

Clearing the circle, Kendall kept her shield up around her. Tonight just seemed darker than other nights. Kam was right about leaving her here. She had a feeling that Alistair and his group of maniacs were up to no good right now. She only hoped that the patrol would keep them from bringing their dark magic to the area. There were enough dark casters already. The balance in Witch's Hollow was already struggling. Maybe it was time to send some white light out to the world? She'd make sure to mention that to Amber Knight the next time she saw her. If the light workers banded together, then they might be able to replenish some energy.

A loud crash against the cabin made her jump. "What the hell?"

Kendall was afraid to look outside. She'd watched enough horror movies to know that going to check on something like that was a mistake. She picked up her phone and dialed Kam's number. She wasn't even sure that he would be able to answer his phone right now, especially if he had shifted. Something slammed against the door, and Kendall bolted for the bedroom. She curled up in the closet and closed her eyes.

Kam. She called out for him, praying that her thoughts would reach him. *Help!*

Kendall closed her eyes and said every prayer she had. She heard something scrape along the outside of the window of the room, and her eyes flew open. Kam had told her to stay inside and to not unlock the door for any reason. What if that didn't keep whoever that was out of the cabin? What if it was a creature sent from the dark casters? Was that a door she heard rattling?

Kam!

Loud howls could be heard on the horizon. She prayed that Kam was on his way with back up. She had no idea what was out there, and while she wanted to take Alistair down, there was still a fair amount of fear where he was concerned. Kendall put her head in her lap and tried to shut out the dark thoughts that rose to her mind. Alistair was near. She felt him, but not near enough to put himself at risk, that she was sure enough. In this situation, he was bound to have one of his lackeys taking care of it. Still, she had no idea what kind of people he ran with right now. They could be far worse than the group he had before.

Kendall heard the front door slam open and tried to keep herself from bolting out of her spot. She heard an unfamiliar voice call out. "Come out, come out, wherever you are."

Closing her eyes, she let loose a litany of words that would help disguise her energy. Then she waved her hands over her and used the only other spell she knew. Now camouflaged, she looked just like the wall behind her. All she had to do was keep her mouth shut and keep herself from moving. "Goddess protect me," she whispered.

The man came into the room, his boots clunking on the ground like drum beats. He jerked open the closet door and peered inside. His eyes looked over every inch of the space, and Kendall held her breath. The man closed the doors and muttered something she could not hear. When he finally moved away, she let her breath out as slowly as she could so as not to draw any attention to herself. She would have to keep this up as long as she could until help arrived. *Please let help be on its way.*

As the man left the room, she heard a low snarl that she recognized. She almost breathed a sigh of relief when she heard several padded feet behind his. The next few moments were filled with snarls and bone crunching that she could hear from there. When the flurry of activity stopped, she heard Kam's voice. "Check outside for more."

She heard him step into the room, but couldn't see anything from the closet doors. When the doors opened to reveal Kam's concerned face, Kendall snapped her fingers and let her disguise fade. She launched herself into his arms. "Kam!"

"Thank God!" Kam held her tight against him and kissed the top of her head. "I got here as soon as you called."

"Is he...?"

"Gone."

"Will he be back?" she asked fearfully.

"Not in this lifetime." His voice was gruff. "The boys will have to clean up the mess. We can't stay here."

Kendall shivered at the imagery that popped into her head. "Does that happen often?"

"Are you asking how many men we've killed?" Kam asked her.

"I.... No, I don't need to know that." Kendall shivered slightly.

"Does it disgust you?" he asked her softly.

"No. He had it coming. If he'd found me...." Kendall did not finish that thought.

"That was one hell of a spell, by the way."

Kam was visibly impressed when she looked up at him. "It's nothing, really."

"Seriously? Kendall, if you hadn't cast it—"

"I know, Kam. I did what you told me to. I stayed put."

"He must want you more than we thought. We'll have to keep you protected at all times, Kendall."

"What? You can't have me followed twenty-four hours a day, Kam. That's not possible. You have work to do. So do the rest of them, and they have their own families to protect. We'll have to find another way."

Kendall was not going to let him bulldoze her on this one. With her being connected to the Knight family now, Alistair would know. There was no going back from here. She couldn't just cast a binding spell and hope he decided to leave them alone. Alistair would never fall for that. No, something else would have to be done. What, she did not know yet.

"What do you suggest?" Kam asked her.

"We need to speak with the witches, Kam."

"The camp?" He looked as if that were the last place he wanted to go.

"Yes. We're going tomorrow." Kendall put her foot down. This was going to be the first of many arguments she would win. Especially if she got Amber Knight on board. "Where are we going to sleep tonight?"

"There's always a room free at the inn."

"Good, I'd like to spend some time with your mother."

"You — Really?"

"What's so bizarre about that?" She glared up at him.

"You were so afraid of her earlier."

"Pfft. Nonsense. She's a lovely woman. And smart too."

"To Knight's Orchard it is then." He started to lead her from the room. "Just close your eyes here, will you?"

"You got it."

Kendall did as he asked. She did not need to see a mangled body at all. That was something she could go a lifetime without seeing. Hopefully, she would be able to get some kind of sleep tonight. She had a feeling she was going to need it for tomorrow.

CHAPTER 15

When they reached Knight's Orchard, Kendall was half asleep. She could officially chalk this up as the longest day ever. As they made their way up the small walkway to the bed and breakfast, Kendall breathed a sigh of relief. It was clear to see that this property was surrounded by a strong protection spell. She sensed Amber's energy and smiled. Kam was right to bring her here. She immediately felt safer.

Amber Knight threw the door open and pulled Kendall into a warm hug. "Oh, child. You must be terrified."

Kendall tried to shake off the tears that threatened to fall, but she was too tired to keep them at bay. She had spent what felt like a lifetime trying to be strong and pretend that Alistair's control over her did not bother her. His talons had ripped into her soul in the most horrific ways. She had been so busy trying to survive that Kendall had not really processed her feelings.

"I'm okay," she tried to answer.

Amber looked up at Kam. "I've got her. Go do what you need to do, Kameron."

"Kameron?" Kam chuckled slightly. "She only uses that when she's about to put her foot down."

"She needs some rest. You do not need to get her upset all over again." Amber's voice brokered no argument.

Kendall closed her eyes and willed the tears to stop. She walked over to Kam and kissed him on the cheek. "I'm fine, Kam. Just need some sleep."

"I'll be back as soon as we're done." Kam kissed the top of her forehead and stroked his hand against her back.

"I know," she whispered. "I love you."

Kam put his head on hers. "I love you too, Kendall."

Kendall sighed as he pulled away from her. As dark as the world seemed, she still had one bright light to help her through. She watched him leave, praying that nothing else happened that night. Alistair would not be happy that he'd lost one of his cronies. For now, he probably hadn't realized that he was dead. Part of her hoped it would send a message that she was off limits. The rest of her knew it would do the opposite. Alistair liked a good challenge, and he was still pissed off that she had run from him in the first place. How was she ever going to get him out of her life? The answer was simple, really, but not something she could actually live with. Alistair had to die. That was the only way she would ever be free, and the only way she could keep him from killing another witch.

"Come, sit." Amber reached out her hand to touch Kendall's.

Kendall followed Amber to the couch near the fireplace. She sat down beside her and stared down at her hands. Squeezing her eyes shut, she tried to figure out what to say. Guilt filled every inch of her. She had brought this evil to this family. If Kam had stayed away from her, his family would not be dealing with this. What would she do if Alistair hurt Kam or any of his family?

"I'm sorry," Kendall whispered.

"Nonsense, child. You have nothing to be sorry for." Amber put her hand on Kendall's shoulder.

"I brought this here." Tears fell from her eyes as she thought about all the things that Alistair was capable of.

Amber shook her head. "You did not bring him here, Kendall."

"He's been looking for me."

"That may very well be, but that did not make him kill the others. You have no reason to feel guilty about that."

"I couldn't save them."

Squeezing her eyes shut, she remembered the cages in the dungeon, filled with women who had been manipulated and tortured into thinking they belonged there. No one deserved to be stuck inside that dark hell hole, no matter what they had done before they were taken there. Alistair had preyed on her guilt, sensing her anger at her sister. He had never known the real reason for her sadness. Kendall had felt guilty for pining after a man that did not belong to her. She would have given every fantasy up just to have her sister by her side. Being young and naïve, she had fallen for what looked like protection and love. That changed far too quickly, but she had already been in too deep.

"No. You couldn't. You cannot save those that are unwilling to be saved." Amber sighed. "You are not the only one to survive such a fate. There's another witch in the camp who has gone through the same thing you have. Ginger was a captive too."

"To Alistair?"

"No, to another dark caster, the one who trained Alistair. His name was Declan."

"Was?"

"He got his, Kendall, just as Alistair will. We're a powerful lot when you stack us all together," Amber assured her.

Did she dare hope that he had suffered a dire fate? Was that so wrong? Harm none, lest ye be harmed. Why was it that it only seemed to work for those who followed that creed? There were so many people in this world who disregarded it. Their crimes against humanity seemed to go unnoticed. How did they not realize they were tearing their world apart? It didn't take a genius to see it. Choosing to be blind to the evils of the world was something Kendall refused to do. While it would be easier to float in a bubble, ignoring the darkness that had infiltrated their world, Kendall could not be a part of that ilk any longer. She had been doing that for the past few years since she had broken free from Alistair's control.

Unfortunately, that had not happened soon enough to save her father from his fate. Kendall would always regret putting him through hell. At the time, Kendall had not been able to see anything but her own pain. She had not realized that her choices had broken her father's heart. He had lost both of his daughters. Kendall had tried to make her peace with it, but deep down, it would always be there with her. At least she had not wasted any more time with her mother. While their relationship was still strained, Kendall had at least been able to be there for her mother when she needed her. Whether that was enough, she would never truly know. Their relationship had never been close. Maybe it was because

Kendall was nothing like the child her mother had hoped she would be. All their hopes had been put on Hannah. Very little was left for her.

Kendall shook those thoughts away. They were a remnant from a time she would have to move past. Kendall could not afford to let herself spiral. That would not help anyone. Part of her knew that they only existed to torment her. That was part of Alistair's psychological hold on her. She could feel him pushing into her mind. Shivering, she put her hand on Amber's hand. "How can we do that? He's grown stronger. I can feel it."

"He's no match for all of us, Kendall. Don't you worry."

She closed her eyes and tried to fight the exhaustion of the day. A yawn escaped her before she could stop it. "Goodness. Excuse me."

"You must be exhausted. You've had a busy couple of days. Let's get you to your room." Amber stood and nodded for her to follow her.

"I hate to be so much trouble."

Kendall was used to taking care of herself, but suddenly she felt as if her life was out of her control. Letting other people help her simply had not been something she had been able to do before. Maybe it was time to trust someone and take the leap of faith required to let them in. Look where it had gotten her with Kam. She looked down at the ring and smiled. Had his mother even noticed? Probably not, but there was time to tell her later. Right now, sleep was definitely calling her name.

"This is the pink room. I hope you like it." Amber pushed open the door.

Kendall smiled as she looked around. When Amber had said pink room, she had expected a pale pastel princess room. She was surprised to find the room was filled with different shades of pink. The curtains were white with pink roses accentuated with the green leaves that surrounded them. There were gold metal butterflies on the wall that were beautiful accents. Kendall wasn't sure that pink would be a color she would have in her house, but it was pretty soothing. The best part was the plush comforter on the bed. It made it look warm and inviting.

"It's beautiful."

"Thank you. Brina helped me redecorate it a few years ago. The girls like to stay here sometimes. They love to have princess slumber parties."

"They're adorable girls."

Kendall smiled as she thought about how much she would love to get to know them better. She didn't want to overstep, though. Only time would tell how well she adjusted to family life with the Knight pack. They were all bigger than life, and she was so...she wasn't quite sure what or who she was really. That was something she would be working out.

"Yes, they are. A handful sometimes, but we do the best we can with them. They often get overlooked with the babies around."

"It must feel that way sometimes. I hope I can help."

Kendall knew what it was like to be pushed to the side. How many dance recitals had her parents missed while they were off at one of Hannah's basketball games? When it wasn't basketball, it was softball. Hannah was a star on every team. Kendall hadn't even been on a competitive dance team, not because she had not been good enough, but because Kendall hated competition. There was always someone feeling like a loser at the end of the day. She had not wanted to be that person. It would only have disappointed her parents even more.

"I'm sure you can. Why don't we have a play date tomorrow? It's Saturday, so Taela will be out of school. Sophie's in her last year of preschool. She'll be a kindergartener next year. I can't believe it. Time sure flies." Amber seemed almost wistful. It made Kendall feel guilty that she might not be able to give her more grandchildren to spoil.

"You love them very much, don't you?" Kendall asked softly.

"Of course I do. Grandchildren, they make the world a better place." Amber answered her with a bright smile, but when she noticed the sadness on Kendall's face, she looked thoughtful. "You seem troubled, dear."

"It's just...." Her lips trembled slightly. "I may never have children."

"Hush now, child. You cannot predict the future." Amber waved her words away.

"And if I can't?"

"You're still my daughter. And Kam will still love you." Amber walked over and wrapped her in a warm hug. "You'd be surprised how much love we have to share, Kendall. You just have to let us."

"I'll try." She smiled weakly at her. "I just don't want to disappoint anyone."

"Don't you worry about that. The only thing I care about is my son's happiness. He's happier than I've seen him in years,

Kendall, and you're the reason. So, don't worry yourself about what could be. Just think about what you have right now."

"You're right."

Kendall sniffed slightly. Amber was right. Dwelling on something that hadn't even happened was not going to help her right now. It was just a deflection, keeping her from focusing on what needed to be done next. For now, she would keep her thoughts to herself about what they needed to do next. She had a feeling they would be discussing that in the morning anyway. She could see the exhaustion on Amber's face.

"We're both tired. I think it's time for bed."

"I'm just down the hall if you need me. Kenton is here too. You'll be perfectly safe here." Amber's eyes were filled with resolve.

"Thank you."

Kendall watched Amber walk from the room and sighed in relief when she was finally alone again. She liked the woman, but Kendall really needed to regroup her thoughts. That, and she was ready to fall asleep on her feet. She took off her socks and shoes and slid underneath the covers. Tomorrow she would have Kam bring her some of her clothes. Eventually, she hoped they would be able to stay at their house. To do so, Kendall would have to make a lot of decisions. It would be nice to throw herself into that, so she didn't have to think about the lunatic that was tearing apart the peaceful balance of Witch's Hollow. Kendall would do whatever she could to resolve this issue, even if it meant getting blood on her own hands.

CHAPTER 16

When light started to stream through the window the next morning, Kendall felt its warmth on her skin. Opening her eyes, she almost forgot where she was. Then she remembered what had happened the night before. The reality of her situation sank in, and she made a fist. If Alistair thought he was going to ruin her life, he had another thing coming. No way was she going to sit back and let him throw his weight around the world. She should have stopped him before, but looking back, she realized that she had not had the strength she had right now. Kendall would not stop until his power had been completely removed. That was the only way the women he held would be free.

The only problem was, where did she start? When she had cast her binding spell on him before, she had only managed to keep him away from her. There were many more women who needed to be protected from him. Where was he hiding them now? Were they back in the other building? Or had he found a new place to hide them from the world? If what Amber had said was true, it was entirely possible that there was an entire ring that needed to be taken down. How were they going to find it? A tracking spell? Would that even work? Magic could be tricky. There were so many things that could go wrong, and very little promises that it would lead her down the right path. Especially with the darkness that cycled around them.

Kendall sat up and stretched. Her entire body felt sore as if she'd run a marathon while carrying a load of bricks on her back. Had it been the sex? Or was it the stress from the day before bleeding into her muscles? Pushing up out of the bed, she ran her fingers through her hair, trying to contain the tangles before they were completely out of control. With none of her things here, she would have to make do. Kendall put her socks and shoes back on, wishing she had a fresh pair on hand. Maybe she could have Kam retrieve some of her things later. She didn't want to return to the cabin. Kendall shivered at the thought of the gruesome sight that would be laying inside the living room. She was not a fan of blood, especially when it meant that her mate had ripped him to shreds. Kendall didn't have to be in the room when it happened. Kam's protective nature would have kicked in, driving him to do whatever he had to do to keep her safe. Had the man even realized what he was stepping into? Or had Alistair led him into the wolf's den without giving him all the details?

That made her wonder how much Alistair knew about her mate and the Knight family. Was he aware that he was up against a fierce pack of werewolves? Would he use that knowledge to bring the outside world down upon their heads? Kendall had lived in the next town over most of her life, and had never heard about werewolves in the area before. Then again, no one really knew much about the magical community either. A lot of the towns were split between their religious beliefs, with very little room for anything outside their secular realms. Whether people believed in magic or not did not matter. It still existed regardless of what people believed, in ways they would never truly understand. The energy in nature around them was powerful. It helped fuel the magic that pumped through her veins.

How was she going to keep the Knight family safe from a predator like Alistair? This wasn't going to be easy. She was going to need as much help as she could get. First, she would talk to Amber. They needed to bring as many of the witches under their wing as possible. Maybe they could help her locate him. Then they could make a plan of action. Binding him, that was the first step. Freeing the women, that was the second step. If they could remove his powers, they would be able to get the women to leave. That in itself would put him out of business, so to speak. Then Kendall could put the past behind her.

After refreshing herself in the bathroom in the hall, Kendall made her way downstairs, where the delicious smell of bacon wafted to her nose.

"Mmmmm...that smells divine."

"So do you."

Kendall squeaked. "Kam. You scared me."

He smiled ruefully at her. "Sorry."

She pouted her lips. "Liar."

"Hey now. I even brought some doughnuts. Be nice, or I'm taking them back."

"Give me!" She moved around him and went in search of the sugary delicacies. When she walked into the dining room, she saw two little faces smiling at her.

"Auntie Kendall!" Sophie hopped up from the chair and

launched herself at her.

Kendall almost had the air knocked out of her. She knelt down and wrapped her arms around her. "Good morning to you too, bug!"

"Bug? Ewww, I'm not a bug." Sophie wrinkled her nose.

"You look like a ladybug to me." Kendall ruffled her hair lovingly and shooed her to the table. "Looks like we've got a lot of food to eat today."

"And Uncle Kam brought doughnuts too!" Taela exclaimed. Her mouth was covered in chocolate icing from the doughnut she was devouring.

"I can see that. Did you save any for me?" she asked her.

"There are tons of them. Look, this one has jelly in it." Sophie pointed to the end of the sugar crusted doughnut, where a red goo was sticking out of it.

"That looks yummy."

"You can have it if you want. I already have mine." Sophie held up the doughnut on her plate.

"Why, thank you. Can I sit next to you, bug?"

"Sure." Sophie patted the chair next to her.

Kendall wiped away some of the sugar the child had gotten on the chair before she sat down. She saw the gentle love on Kam's face and knew he was just as entranced by his nieces as she was. Reaching over, she picked up the doughnut and took a small bite. Closing her eyes, she savored the sweet sugary dough. She couldn't remember the last time she'd had a jelly doughnut. When she opened her eyes, she saw a golden heat in Kam's eyes. Kendall blushed and looked away. When she realized she had gotten some of the jelly on her fingers, she licked it off. This time she knew better than to look up at him. She felt his heat from there.

"These are delicious." Kendall almost picked up another, but she wanted to try some of the other food. She loaded up her plate with eggs, bacon, and a few slices of toast.

"I'll have to get some more." He smiled secretively.

Kendall wondered what his mind was up to, but she didn't have to wonder for long, for his thoughts were soon made known.

I'd lick them off every inch of your body.

Kendall shivered and nibbled on her bottom lip. *That sounds delicious.*

"So, what are we going to do today?" Taela asked her.

"What would you like to do today?" Kendall had no plans. She hadn't planned on spending all day with them, but how could she resist their charm?

"You only get her for the morning. Then she's all mine," Kam interrupted.

"Uncle Kam!!" complained Sophie.

"We've got a lot of work to do if we're going to get the house in order," Kam explained.

"He's right, girls. I have a lot of things to pick. Should we paint a room for the girls?" asked Kendall. She wouldn't mind having a place for the girls to come visit.

"Oh, can we help?" Taela's eyes lit up with excitement.

"Tell you what—I'll have Kendall pick out a few colors, and then the two of you can vote on which color we pick," Kam promised them.

"No boy colors." Sophie turned up her nose in disgust.

"Sounds fair." Kendall would make sure to pick a few that the girls would like. Maybe they could get a few bunk beds for the room. That would save some room while giving them the perfect play space. If she played her cards right, Kam would let her do whatever she wanted to. It was clear how much he loved the girls. His nephews too. Kam was an exceptionally caring man. He may not look like it under that gruff exterior.

"So, what are we going to do this morning then?" Taela asked curiously.

"I don't know. What do you like to do?" Kendall waited for them to answer.

"Um...we like to play games, paint, and make things," Sophie answered. "Do you know how to paint, Auntie?"

"I do, bug." Kendall smiled. She couldn't remember the last time she had painted anything, but art had always been one of her favorite subjects. Outside of music, that was.

"Yay! Can we paint, Nana?" Sophie asked Amber as she walked into the room.

"Maybe, but we have to change your clothes."

"Why?" pouted Sophie. "I like this dress."

"Me too, but you don't want to get paint on it, do you?" Kendall pointed out.

"Oh, right. Okay, but I want to put it back on when we're done." The four-year-old was quite logical in her thinking.

"Now, let's eat, girls." Amber nodded to the food.

The meal was filled with squeals and laughter as the girls continued with their antics. They were so innocent and filled with life. Kendall was almost taken back to another time and place when she and her sister had been like two peas in a pod. Kendall had followed her sister everywhere. At the time, Kendall hadn't realized how annoying that had to be, but

Hannah had never turned her away. Her sister was a saint to put up with her. She imagined Taela had the same role here. Sophie reminded her a lot of herself when she was that age. If only she had maintained her innocence, the world wouldn't feel as dark as it did right now. The fact that the girls were oblivious to the dangers around them was a miracle. It really reflected the magic that surrounded them, sheltering them from the things no children should be exposed to.

When they were finished eating their breakfast, the girls helped their grandmother do dishes while Kam pulled her outside for a walk. Kendall didn't say anything as their feet moved across the grass. She wasn't sure what there was to say. Their circumstances had changed slightly. Not because of what he had done last night, but because she carried such guilt for making him a part of it.

"Kam—" she started to say.

"I'm sorry, Kendall," Kam interrupted her.

"What?" She turned to look at him. "What do you have to be sorry for?"

"I left you unprotected." Fear and regret were shadowed in his eyes.

Kendall smiled at him and put a hand on his face. "None of this is your fault, Kam. In fact, if I had never—"

"Don't say that," he warned her.

"But—"

"No regrets, Kendall. I won't let you fill your head with them." Kam pulled her into his arms, and his mouth came down to hers. The gentle love that flowed from his lips to hers took her breath away. It was as if he were begging her to stay when she had no need to flee.

She broke the kiss and held her hand up. "Kam. I'm not going anywhere, but the truth of the matter is, I brought this man into the equation here. If I had never met him—"

"You wouldn't be here with me," Kam pointed out.

"How do you know that?"

"Because all roads lead to our future, Kendall. The road you took led you to me." He seemed so sure of himself.

"And if I had not been fooled by him, then what?"

"You might have married some puny accountant, and not felt like you could have more than what was standing right before you."

"How do you mean?"

"Your anger made you fight for what you wanted," he answered matter-of-factly.

He was right. The anger had been there when she was younger, but not to the extent it had grown to once her life had been marred by her time with Alistair. She may not be proud of that time, but she had survived it. Kendall had worked hard to erase his narrative from her mind. She was still a work in progress, but she was fiercely determined to do better with this life she had now.

"All I ever wanted was love, Kam."

It was true. Her parents' love, her sister's. His. They were the only things that had ever mattered to her, but her fear of it had kept her from remembering it. She had spent so much time blaming herself for everything that she hadn't stopped to remind herself that there were good things to remember. Her jealousy of her sister, it made her sad, but it was also a part of life. Sibling rivalry happened in every household. So did mistakes, in some more than others. While she had been so wrapped up in her own feelings, she didn't realize she had everything she wanted until it was almost too late. Now, she had Kam and his wonderful, albeit loud and overreaching, family. But they were perfectly imperfect.

"You are loved, more than you know." His voice was soft and endearing.

"You're not getting mushy on me, are you?" she teased him.

"That depends."

"On what?" Kendall asked him curiously.

"If it's working in my favor." He winked at her, and she saw the golden flash in his eyes.

"Kameron Knight! This is not the time or place for that," she chastised him.

"I know, but he has a mind of his own, unfortunately."

"Well, tell him he's waited this long, a few more hours are not going to kill him." She slapped his hand away before it could reach for her breasts. Shaking a finger at him, she shook her head. "I have to paint with the girls."

"I know. I need to take a look at one of the properties. Be ready for lunch?" He asked her, hopefully.

"Yes, and then we have a lot of work to do, right?"

"Yes...work." He grinned at her. "Oh, here comes the princess squad. Looks like it's my turn to run while I still can."

Kendall saw the girls running toward her. Their bright smiles could light up the darkest day. She turned away from Kam and started back toward the house. Part of her wanted to leave with Kam right now, but the rest of her knew it would have to wait. As much as she joked about his desire, he had but to look at her to gain her interest. Every inch of her wanted to explore his body in ways she couldn't even understand yet. Maybe someday she would figure it out. For now, she was going to push all her thoughts from her head and focus on spending time with two rays of sunshine.

CHAPTER 17

When Kam returned to pick her up, Kendall was wiping away the rest of the paint from her hands. She smiled at him when he walked into the room. "Hello, handsome."

He stepped over to her and his thumb smoothed over her cheek. "You missed a spot."

"Thanks."

She reached up and kissed him on the mouth. One thing was for sure, she liked having someone to love. He made her feel at peace even when her thoughts were out of control when he wasn't around. At least the girls had kept her in the moment. They were like a healing balm. Their innocence was soothing.

"Are you ready to go?" He asked her.

"Yes. Where are we going?"

"Furniture shopping." He grinned at her.

"Oh?"

"It has come to my attention that I need a bed."

"Bed?"

Kam brought his face closer to her ear and whispered, "Unless you want carpet burn."

"Oh...right." She shivered at the images that his words

put in her head. "You don't suppose they have same day delivery, do you?"

"I'd pay extra for it."

Kendall giggled as she followed him out the door. She wondered how many things he'd let her pick out. They did have an entire house to furnish. It wasn't like she was attached to any of her things, really. The only thing she would want to keep was the hope chest that had belonged to Hannah. Getting rid of her mother's things had been so much easier. Her mother had told her to keep only the things that were special to her. There was no need to hang onto things that would only clutter up her life. Her mom had been right to a certain extent. Sometimes she did want to remember her mother — not how their relationship had become, but the way it had been when she was a child before Kendall started to form a jealousy of her sister. That seemed like forever ago, but she was working on remembering it.

Part of her problem was that the darkness that Alistair had brought to her life had amplified her angst and anger. This had almost obliterated any happy thoughts from her mind. Only time would tell if she were able to retrieve some of them. Kendall refused to give up. Looking over at Kam, she realized he was a big part of her restoration. She was like his next project, whether he realized it or not. Poor man had his work cut out for him, that was for sure.

When they arrived at the furniture store, Kendall's eyes were wide like a child at Christmas. Everything was so beautiful and well made. The problem was it was also very expensive. She looked at the price tag to an oak table and put her hand on her chest. "Oh my lord, this is — "

"Price is not a problem, Kendall," he assured her.

She shook her head. "You don't keep money by spending it, Kam. There's no need to go for the most expensive item."

"Kendall, you have to trust me." He put his hands on her shoulders and started to knead the tight muscles. "Tell me what you like."

Somehow Kendall thought he was talking about something else altogether, but she refused to call him out on it right now. Instead, she would take a closer look at the furniture. If he refused to go on a budget, then she would at least make sure that the quality was worth the money. Running her hand along a mahogany table, she smiled. She had always liked the darker woods, and it would go well with the floors. If they chose the oak, it would not look right. While the walls would be lighter, they would have the right contrast with the dark wood. "I like the color, but not the chairs."

"All right. What about that one?"

Kendall looked to where he pointed, and her eyes lit up. The beautifully carved chairs reminded her of the forest. Each back had leaves etched into the top. Walking over to it, she tried one of the seats out and was surprised at how comfortable they were. "I like this set."

"Good. Me too." He had an amused smile on his face.

"What's so funny?" She asked him.

"I can get this at almost no cost," he grinned.

"Why's that?"

"Killian made them."

"What?" She ran her fingers around the carvings. "He builds houses and makes furniture? Is there anything he can't do?"

"Apparently not. I'm sure he would be happy to gift a set to us."

"No!" Kendall held her hand up in protest. "Don't tell him. He should get paid for his masterpiece."

"Perhaps."

"Besides, you said money was not a problem." She put her hands on her hips, and her chin jutted out in challenge.

"Very well. Should we get the rest of the set?"

Kendall looked at the matching cabinetry. Each one had the same minute details as the chairs and legs of the table. "Can we?"

"I don't see why not. Although I'll never hear the end of it." Kam's eyes had a merry shine.

"You'll get over it. Besides, it's better made than the rest of those." She nodded to the more expensive pieces.

"True."

Kendall stepped closer to him and whispered in his ears. "It has to hold our weight if we're going to christen the dining room."

Kam's breath caught in his throat, and a low growl left his mouth. "Woman, you are playing with fire."

"Didn't you say something about a bed?" Kendall reminded him.

"Yes, but so help me, if you buy one he carved...."

"It's not like he'll actually be there with us when you—"

"Damn it, Kendall. That hadn't occurred to me. We might not be able to use that table after all," he grumbled against her.

"Nonsense. I'm sure you'll come around," she whispered in his ear.

"Oh.... I see what you did there. Very clever, Kendall." Kam sighed. "Let's get this over with so we can at least get a bedroom set delivered."

"Will we be safe there?" Kendall didn't want to ask that question, but she needed to know. She didn't want to bring Alistair down upon the house they would call home.

"Yes. Not to worry. I've had the land blessed and protected. He shouldn't be able to track you there, Kendall."

She nodded at him. She wasn't sure if she could believe that for sure. All she could do was hope that what he said was true. Kendall would also do what she could to put up her own spell of protection around it. There was still so much that needed to be done, but part of her felt guilty for taking this small interlude with her mate. She told herself that life had to go on, whether Alistair was there or not.

Kendall walked over to the bedroom furniture and looked through all the sets. She had a few that she was interested in, but it wasn't until she saw the four-poster bed that Kendall knew she had found the perfect set. Her mind turned to all the things they could do with those posts, which made that bed the only contender.

She saw that Kam was having similar thoughts. "Are you thinking what I'm thinking?"

"I'm not telling." His voice was a little gruff, but his eyes spoke volumes.

"I like this one too. Nice secure." She let her words end there and saw the golden light glowing in his eyes. Kendall laid down on the bed and looked to make sure no one else was watching. Spreading her arms over her head, she saw that there was plenty of room in between the posts for her arms to be open wide. Patting the bed beside her, she waved Kam over to her. "Try out this mattress."

Kam was reluctant to sit down beside her, but he gave in to her regardless. He lay down next to her and bounced the bed up slightly. The springs squeaked under him. "This one's too noisy."

"Agreed. And a little too soft, if you ask me. The harder, the better."

"Kendall...I think there are some words you might need to exclude from your vocabulary." His words were a warning.

"Harder?" she asked him innocently.

"Precisely. Pretty sure it can't get much harder," he grumbled.

"Poor, sweet baby." She consoled him with her hand on his shoulder. "Let's try all the mattresses out."

"This was a bad idea," he muttered.

"Oh, shush. The faster we pick it, the faster it can be delivered, right?"

"If I have to call my brothers, that bed will be there today." He grinned as he followed her to the next mattress.

For the next hour, Kendall picked everything she wanted for the house for the time being. They didn't need to furnish everything, just enough to get the house open. The painting could be done a room at a time if they needed. Or not at all. The white walls would certainly work for now. There would be time to do the rest a little at a time. She was looking forward to moving into the house as soon as possible. They may not have everything sorted, but at least they would have more privacy there than they would have at the inn.

"Now that we're done, let's eat," Kam suggested.

"I like how you think, sir." For some reason, Kendall was starving. Maybe it was the excitement of the morning or leftovers from the day before. She couldn't pinpoint it exactly. Not that it mattered.

Kam drove her to a Chinese buffet, much to her surprise. Her eyes lit up, and she clapped her hands. "I love this place! I used to come here all the time with —"

"Hannah told me about it. Strange how we were never here at the same time."

"Definitely. It's hard to believe we were just a few miles away from each other this whole time. The world is a small place sometimes, isn't it?"

"Agreed. Maybe we can get some to go too. That way, we have some left for dinner tonight," Kam suggested.

"Sounds good to me." Kendall saw the sign that indicated they should seat themselves. She couldn't fight the urge to find the same booth that had been their favorite. Sliding into the booth, she smiled up at him. "This was our favorite spot."

"I see. Close enough to get easy access to the food, but far enough away to give you some privacy from the line of people."

"Exactly." Kendall beamed at him. "I wish Hannah were here with us."

"Maybe she is," he suggested.

She smiled at him. "You're right. She probably is. Do you think she's okay with us?"

"What do you think, Kendall?" He asked her quietly. Kam's face had changed since she brought her up.

Kendall put her hand on his. "Hannah was many things, Kam. She was not the kind of girl to hold a grudge. I know she cared about you a lot, but she would have wanted you to be happy."

"And you too. Hannah was always talking about the games you used to play when you were younger. Something about you cheating at Battleship."

Kendall looked at the table and averted her gaze. "Only a couple of times."

Kam chuckled. "Right. You say that now, but she seemed to think the only way you won was through cheating."

"Not true," she protested with a grin. She sighed and smiled thoughtfully. "Thank you, Kam."

"For what?" he asked her softly.

"For helping me remember the good times, and giving me so many more to look forward to."

"Speaking of which, let's make our plates. I've got a couple of plans I'm looking forward to tonight." He winked at her.

"Fine." She giggled and shook her head. For the next hour, Kendall tried everything she wanted. Her thoughts were only on Kam and what he had up his sleeve. They would have to get back soon to be there for the bed delivery. The rest of the furniture would be delivered tomorrow. She made the resolution to not think about Alistair and his dark order for the rest of the night. Tomorrow that would be a totally different story.

CHAPTER 18

When they returned to the new house, Kendall was far past stuffed. She couldn't remember the last time she had eaten so much food. Being at one of her favorite places had brought back a piece of Hannah that Kendall had been missing. She had spent so much time feeling guilty about losing Hannah. Everywhere she turned, she seemed to be losing someone. From here on out, she was determined to keep everyone else close to her heart. Living in fear only made it harder to find the silver lining on the darkest clouds.

Kam handed her a key and nodded for her to open the door. She had a feeling he was up to something, but she couldn't quite prove it yet. Kendall opened the door and found a small trail of flower petals. "What is going on, Kam?"

"You'll see." He winked at her as he closed the door behind them.

Kendall followed the trail of flowers up the stairs. When she made her way into the master bedroom, she saw that their bed had already arrived. She turned to look at him in surprise. "How in the world did you get this here already?"

"I have three strong, able bodied brothers available." He grinned.

"And the flowers?" She crossed her arms over her chest.

"Kyle. He's actually a romantic at heart."

"Boloney!" Kendall had a lot of trouble believing that one. Kyle was so contrary that she didn't know how to take him seriously. She imagined everyone felt the same way about him.

"It's true. But then again, he might have done it to mess with me. The idea of me getting laid is hysterical to him, I suppose." He rolled his eyes.

"Getting laid, huh?" Kendall shook her head at him. If he was going to be crass about it, he had his work cut out for him. Besides, her stomach was too full to think about doing anything like that right now anyway.

"A guy can hope, right?" He stepped closer to her, and she held her hand up to stop him.

"We just ate, Kam. Besides, we need to talk." So far, they had talked about everything, but the one thing they kept avoiding.

"Kendall...."

"We can't keep avoiding it. We have to deal with it. Alistair is not going to give up. You can't hide me in a bubble and hope he never finds me. We need to do something about it."

"We are doing something." Kam brushed her words aside.

"Kameron Knight, you are going to listen to me whether you want to or not. I have a plan." Or a facsimile of one. It would take some time and effort from the witch community near Witch's Hollow, as well as manipulating the forces that ran between the ley lines there.

171

"I'm listening." He crossed his arms over his chest and waited to hear what she had to say.

"We need to do a binding spell."

"A binding spell? Is that all?" He looked at her as if she had lost her mind.

"Hear me out, Kam. I'm not sure that our goal should be killing our enemies. Is that the way you settle the score around here?" She asked him curiously.

"No, but if the need calls for it." Kam's voice was almost a grumble.

"Well, if you kill him, you'll not be able to get into his world. His power will just bleed into the next dark caster in line. That's what happened with Declan, right?"

Amber had told her a little more about Declan that morning as they painted. Whenever the girls were preoccupied, the two of them talked about a plan of action. Amber agreed with her assessment of the situation, which made her feel much better about putting the plan into motion. She would not move without Kam on her side, though. She needed to know that he trusted her ability to take care of herself.

"Declan was a horrible man. I imagine Alistair is a lot like him." His fists were clenched at his sides now.

"You really don't like them, do you?"

"Any evil thing that topples the balance of power here is unwelcome in my book. Declan was here for a time before he was taken out."

"What happened to him?" Kendall didn't know what possessed her to ask that question.

"At the time, my father was still alpha of our pack. That was his last battle as leader. He led the charge into Declan's lair. When we tried to infiltrate there, Declan killed the witches he had been controlling. Even in his death, that man acted as if he had won. In many ways, he had. Apparently, his power passed on to the next in line."

"I'm sorry, Kam. That had to be hard to witness." Kendall could only imagine the horrors that Kam had seen, having witnessed a handful of them herself. Her time in the dungeon had been a living nightmare that would follow her around until the day they took Alistair's control away.

"If we bind him, then what, Kendall?"

At least he was listening to her now. He might actually take her seriously, which was a relief. "Then we do a cleansing spell over the witches he is holding captive."

"And how do we find them all?" Kam asked her warily.

"First, we track him."

Kendall did not want to tell him that she would have to be the one to do it. She might even have to become bait in order to get him to show his face. She would definitely have to make herself vulnerable to his attack, but that did not mean she had to leave herself completely wide open. There had to be a failsafe of some kind, and if she could talk to the other witches, she was sure she could come up with a compromise that would make everyone happy.

"As long as that does not put you in danger." Kam seemed to know where her thoughts were headed.

"I don't want to be in danger either, but the only way we'll get his scent is if he gets close to me, Kam. We have to lure him closer."

"I don't like it. Not at all." Kam was now stone faced.

"Damn it, Kam. I want a future with you. I can't have it if

he is out there ready to destroy it."

"And if he destroys you?" Kam's voice was almost afraid.

"Have a little faith in me, Kam. Have a little faith in all of us. We can do this. I know we can." Kendall reached out to touch his face. "I'm not going to leave you, Kam. Our love is stronger than this darkness. Love is one of the most powerful things in the world. We can overcome this."

"It goes against every inch of my conscience to let you put yourself up as bait, Kendall."

"I know, love."

Kendall put her head on his chest and breathed in his earthy scent. Strong arms wrapped around her, and Kendall was resolved to keep them there no matter the cost. When his hands started to massage her back, a tingling feeling raced through her body. No matter how full her stomach was, her body was starving for him. Her mouth came up to his and was not disappointed.

The heat of his kiss was filled with a longing that she understood. He did not want to let her do what needed to be done, but both of them knew there was no choice. When his tongue plunged into hers, she sighed against him, which created a chain reaction she could have almost predicted. Kam deepened the kiss as his hands squeezed her ass. She felt his need circling between them, and she pulled him as close as she could.

Her hands slid down his stomach and unbuttoned his jeans. She broke the kiss and whispered, "Shall we put this bed to the test?"

"I thought you'd never ask." His smile was sexy as hell.

Kendall slid his jeans down his legs, along with his briefs.

When she stood back up, she let her hand graze the tip of his erection before moving up his abdomen and pushing his shirt up over his head. When she was done, she took care of her own clothes. Completely naked before him, she stood there just a foot away, wondering what his first move would be. She didn't have to wait for long.

Kam's arms shot around her and pulled her tight against him as his eyes flashed dangerously. His mouth captured hers with a wildness that had been restricted up to this point. It was a combination of need and desperation. He was a raging fire as his heat took over her. She sighed against him and felt herself tremble in his arms. Kam walked her back toward the bed, and when her legs hit the edge of the bed, he slowly lowered her.

His hands and mouth were suddenly hard to keep track of as he moved up and down the length of her body, conducting her arousal with a wicked rhythm that made it hard to think or breathe. She moaned when he captured her breast with his mouth. Arching into his mouth, she moaned against him.

His voice was shaking. "Do you like that, Kendall?"

"Yes," she whispered. Yes, she liked that very much. Her answer seemed to drive him crazy as he growled against her. His teeth nibbled her nipple gently, and she writhed beneath him.

His hand slid between her legs and started to flick against her clit, and she sighed in ecstasy. He set a pace she could not keep up with. Slow then fast, circular and straight. Kendall tried to focus on his movements, as the sweet desire that had started inside her changed to something almost unreachable. He was mastering her desire, making it build to a fevered pitch. Her breath was coming in slow pants as her hips moved against him. Her orgasm was just out of reach, and he knew it too.

"No finishing, Kendall."

"What?" Her eyes flew open in confusion.

"You heard me. You're not allowed to cum."

"But...," she whimpered. She was already so close to her release that she had to clench her stomach to keep it from pushing past the gates. Sucking in her stomach, Kendall tried to will herself to not think about the finish that she wanted so badly. Unfortunately, her body had a mind of its own and was nearing the finish line when Kam removed his hand. Her insides throbbed painfully, and she tried to still the rhythm of her heart.

"Ah-ah." Kam's mouth covered hers, and his tongue dueled with hers, distracting her briefly from the painful need inside her.

When he replaced his fingers, Kendall sighed, hoping he would finally let her finish, but he repeated the process yet again. She scrunched her stomach tight, trying to rein back the orgasm that threatened to push past her control. "Oh...."

"Not yet, Kendall."

He stopped his movements and bit her nipple to distract her. It did not have the reaction he hoped for, because that one action sent her over the edge and her legs started to jerk on their own accord as a powerful orgasm took her breath away. She sucked in her breath as her control slipped completely. "Please," she begged him.

"Poor baby." Kam took pity on her and started to move his fingers against her.

"Oh!" Her whole body shook against him, and the lights exploded behind her eyes as she started to feel wild and reckless. When his mouth captured hers, she was like an animal against him. She sucked deep into his mouth, trying to pull every inch of his tongue into her.

Kam growled against her and forced her legs open wider. He slid his hot cock into her silky core. "God, you feel good."

Kendall whimpered against him as he pumped slowly in and out of her. Her insides were burning up as he pushed her further past her limits. When he sensed another orgasm coming, he pulled out and chuckled when she hit him with her fists.

"Damn you, Kameron Knight."

"Trust me, Kendall. The end will be so much sweeter."

Or painful, she thought to herself. Right now, every inch of her ached for his touch, missing the warmth of his cock inside her. Kendall squeezed her eyes shut and tried to keep the room from spinning around her. She could honestly say she had never felt this way before. This craziness was taking over every inch of her. She tried to slow her breathing, but as soon as Kam noticed she was trying to calm herself down, he slid back inside her.

"Kam!" Her insides threatened mutiny as he slammed into her a few more times. "I can't...."

"What's the matter, Kendall?" His teeth nibbled her ear lobe as his breath warmed her neck deliciously.

She shivered against him, desire ripping through her like molten lava. Her wild need for him overwrote the rules he had tried to put in place. Her legs wrapped around his ass, pulling him deeper inside her. When he stopped moving, her ass moved off the bed, taking him in and out of her.

"What are you doing, Kendall?" he growled against the breast he had taken into his mouth.

The heat inside her needed to be released. She shut her eyes and ignored his commands. Kendall wanted him more than she wanted the air she breathed. The frenzy could not be turned off. A switch had been pushed inside her, and the narrative could not be rewritten. She didn't care what he said, she was taking what she wanted. Her body wrestled him off her, and she climbed on top of him.

Kam's face was filled with surprise. Clearly, he was not prepared for the animal he had awoken inside her. Kendall slid onto his swollen cock and took what she wanted. At first, she rose up and down in a slow tantalizing rhythm. When that was no longer enough, her fingers scraped against the skin at his chest, and she rode him fast and hard. Kam tried to keep himself still, but even he had his limits. As he slammed in and out of her, she took every inch of it until her insides shook around him.

"That's it baby, cum for me."

His words made her shudder even harder as the fire inside her exploded like fireworks on the fourth of July. She almost collapsed over him, but his hands reached up and gripped her hips. He pulled her up and down on him, taking every inch of her silky core. "God, you feel so good. So soft, so wet."

Kendall's arms reached behind her to steady herself but ended up giving him an entirely new angle that made her eyes fly open. "Oh my!"

Kam's breathing was shallow, and his body went tight beneath her. She could sense his finish, and rather than accommodate him, she pulled herself off him. His eyes flew open and flashed dangerously. His eyes narrowed on her, and a slow grin spread across his face. "The student becomes the teacher?"

"It serves you right, Kameron Knight." Her lips pouted.

"I see." Kameron's hands reached out to tweak her nipples. "Poor baby. And what if I take it?"

"I dare you," she challenged him.

Before she knew it, Kendall was underneath him. Kam pushed her legs apart so far she might as well be doing the splits. He pulled her ass off the bed and slammed into her silky core. His thrust was so far inside her; she thought he would impale her, but she loved every second of it as he stretched her to the limits. At this angle, she could barely move. All she could do was squeeze herself around him and hang on for the ride of her life. Another orgasm ripped through her, and he growled above her. He changed his movement slightly, and she felt his scrotum slapping against her. The added movement made it hard to think. Sanity was overrated anyway.

"Yes!" Kam shouted as he lost his load inside her.

When he finally pulled out of her, Kendall squeezed her legs shut and tried to get the throbbing to stop. It was like a loud, angry beat inside her, having been pushed over the brink with his deliciously talented body. She tried to get her breathing to calm down, but she was having trouble getting any part of her body to listen.

Kam pulled her against him so that her back was against him. "What's the matter, Kendall?"

She took his hand and put it against her clit. "Can you feel that throbbing?"

He kissed her neck, and she could feel his grin. "Poor baby."

"That was amazing," she sighed as he held her close to him.

"Agreed." His hands strummed against her stomach, and she sighed against him.

Yawning, she stretched against him. "I think you're going to put me in a sex coma."

"Then, I succeeded." He chuckled. "Rest, Kendall."

He did not have to tell her twice. She wasn't even sure she would be able to hold her eyes open if she wanted to. Closing her eyes, she recalled every hot moment of their loving and felt like she was floating in a bubble of contentment that not even the darkest night could burst. She felt the covers slide over her as Kam's arms kept her safe and warm against him. She wasn't sure who fell asleep first.

CHAPTER 19

The rest of the day seemed to fade away. When she woke in the morning, she was surprised to find most of her personal items were downstairs in the living room. His brothers must have brought them over through the night. She was thankful that she did not have to return to the cabin. Kendall felt so much safer around here than she ever had at the cabin. She was looking forward to making this their home.

Kendall knew there was a need to find Alistair, but she wasn't quite ready to move on with it. With the Knight pack keeping an eye on the forest, Kendall used the time to get her house in order. Kam seemed content with her nesting drive, mostly because that meant if she were distracted with the house, she would not be going after Alistair. In her way of thinking, the best time to get the strongest binding spell would be to use the next super moon to charge their powers. That was still five weeks away. Kendall hated having to wait so long to act, but Amber Knight had agreed with her. Pushing forward too soon would not make it any easier to remove his powers, so she kept moving forward with life, enjoying her time with Kam with every blissful moment.

The next few weeks passed in a blur as her life took over.

Touching the pentacle at her neck, Kendall smiled softly. Amber had the witches all bless it for her safety. She was thankful for that. It let her breathe a little easier, knowing he would not be able to find her with his magic. Waiting for the time to pass was a lot easier with a house to decorate. Every day she worked on painting a new room. She had even let the girls help paint their room. Life was going as well as could be expected, with only one thing that bothered her. The past few days, she'd had a horrible pain in her side, like a cramp from her cycle that refused to come.

Today she had made an appointment with a gynecologist to see if there was something wrong. Kendall had not wanted to worry Kam with her concerns. It was probably nothing to worry about. Kendall looked around her and smiled. This house was quickly becoming the home of her dreams. Already the walls were filled with enough love to last her a lifetime. She was incredibly lucky. As she opened the door, she took one last look around her before locking the door behind her.

Kendall hopped in her car and turned the key in the ignition. The faint hum of a soft pop song echoed around her. As she drove to the doctor's office, she tried not to worry about things she could not control. Her cycle was like clockwork for the most part. This was the first time she had missed it since.... Kendall shuddered. She did not like to think of that time when Alistair had taken the last bright light from her life. Kendall put a hand to her stomach as a tear fell down her face. That was the last time she thought she could be a mother. His rituals after had ripped her hopes away without a care. She hated him for that, and for so many other things.

As she pulled into the parking lot, Kendall put her head

on the steering wheel. Those thoughts they did not belong in this time and place. Taking a deep breath, she reminded herself to not let his darkness push into her peaceful world. She fought to keep the light pushing her forward into the future that she would have with Kam. Looking down at her ring finger, she knew in her heart that if all she ever had was Kam in her life, he was more than enough.

Kendall made her way into the building and checked in with the receptionist. "Good morning. Kendall Pearson for Dr. Lewis."

"Okay. If you could just take this and leave a sample in the restroom inside. Then have a seat." The woman pointed down the hallway.

"Sure." Kendall grabbed the cup and almost groaned. She hated this part. Getting urine into a cup this size was almost an exact science. If she didn't get the right angle, she'd have a mess on her hands, literally. Stepping into the bathroom, she locked it behind her and took care of business. She quickly washed her hands and dried them. When she was done, she opened the metal door where she was supposed to leave it.

She walked back to the lobby and picked up a magazine. The room was pretty full, so she might be here awhile. As she looked around her, she saw women of differing stages of pregnancy. She couldn't help wondering what it would be like to be in their shoes. It wasn't likely to happen with her history. Her own doctor had seen the scarring inside her. Dr. Lewis had to break the news to her gently at the time. Kendall remembered that day like it was tattooed on the back of her hand. Less than likely. At the time, she hadn't realized the ramifications.

That was two years ago. Her mother had talked her into getting herself checked out. At the time, she had not realized her mother's concern wasn't for her childbearing abilities, but the fact that her mother had a tumor on her cervix. The first one did not show signs of cancer. The second one did, and that was why Kendall was afraid of sudden pains in her body. With her mother's history, Kendall could not afford to take any chances.

"Kendall?" a nurse called from the doorway.

She stood up and followed her into a room and set her purse on the floor next to one of the chairs. "You all are pretty busy today."

"Must be close to a full moon. They all come out in droves then." The nurse smiled at her. "So, what seems to be the problem?"

"I've been cramping on the left side. My mother died recently from ovarian cancer."

"So sorry for your loss." The nurse took her blood pressure and checked her temperature. "The doctor will be in soon. Here's a gown. Bottoms off, please. You can leave your socks on. The stirrups are cold sometimes."

"Thank you."

As soon as the nurse left the room, Kendall got herself ready to see the doctor. She folded her pants and underwear on the chair against the wall. Then she took the paper and covered her legs. Shivering slightly, Kendall sat on the small exam table, crossed her legs, and looked down at the floor. This time, the doctor did not take a lifetime to enter the room.

"Good morning, Kendall. How are you feeling?" Dr. Lewis smiled at her. She was one of the most understanding doctors that Kendall had ever met.

"I'll feel better when I know what's going on with me."

She bit her bottom lip nervously. All kinds of scenarios were racing through her mind. She was not prepared to deal with cancer. Kendall was too young to leave Kam behind.

"Well, I think I can give you a little relief. Your test came back positive." Dr. Lewis was still looking down at her file.

"For what?" Kendall asked her in confusion. What had they been testing for?

Dr. Lewis chuckled. "You're pregnant, Kendall."

"Maybe you should check that again," she argued.

"I'll do one better. Lay back and let's have a look inside."

The doctor reached for a large wand that was covered with what looked like a long condom. She squirted some clear jelly on it and moved toward her. "This is a transvaginal ultrasound. I'm just going to slide this in to get a better look."

Kendall winced as the wand was placed inside her. She watched the screen curiously, wondering what Dr. Lewis would find. When she saw a small circle on the screen, she saw the doctor do a screenshot. "What is that? Is it a tumor?"

"The best kind," teased Dr. Lewis. "Looks like you're six weeks."

Six weeks? How was that possible? She counted back and realized six weeks would be the very night Kam had made her his mate. She had trouble believing it. "But I thought... what about the scarring? Should I be worried about that?"

"Let's take a closer look." The doctor spent the next ten minutes looking around inside her. When she pulled the wand out, she turned to look at her. "Either our first scans were wrong, or your body has somehow found a way to heal itself."

Kendall stared so hard at the screen that her watering eyes forced her to blink. "I don't understand."

"If this was unplanned, you have options," Dr. Lewis said softly.

Options? Was she crazy? This was a dream come true for her, something she hadn't dared to wish for. To have a child of her own, it was almost the perfect ending. If she were lucky enough to fill their house with the love and laughter of their own children, her life would be complete. As much as she had convinced herself that having just Kam was enough, she now realized she wanted more to their lives. Of course, this might also make them race to the altar even faster, but Kendall did not care about a large intricate wedding. Even standing before a justice of the peace would be enough for her.

"It wasn't planned, but it's the most perfect thing ever." Tears slid down her face. "Thank you, Dr. Lewis."

"You're welcome, Kendall. I'll just make you a copy, and I'll have the nurse bring you some information. With your history, I am marking you at risk."

"At risk? Does that mean I'll lose the baby?"

With everything that could go wrong, Kendall was starting to fear the worst case scenario. What if she couldn't carry this baby to term? She would never forgive herself. When should she tell Kam? How could she tell him? They had so much going on right now with trying to take Alistair down that she was afraid he would stop her from acting if he knew about the baby inside her. Yet, there was a huge part of herself that wanted to take herself out of the equation just to protect it.

"No, just that I want to make sure to monitor you closely. It's just a little peace of mind." She reached over to the printer and handed her a small piece of paper. "Here you go. Congratulations."

"Thank you."

Kendall took the paper and traced the outline of the tiny dot that fluttered inside her. She memorized every millimeter of it as she put her hand on her stomach.

The next half hour was a bit of a blur for her as the nurse talked her through the next appointments and the proper nutrition. She still couldn't believe the miracle that was growing inside of her. Where had all her scarring gone? She still had the images from her scan, so it was not like they completely imagined it. How had she been healed? This wasn't normal, that much she was sure of. There was only one person she wanted to talk to about that, and she was no longer here. She had never imagined she would miss her mom like this.

Sometimes she wished she had the ability to hear the dead. Then she could still talk to those that had passed from her life. She wasn't quite sure what Hannah might say to her. Would she be happy to be an aunt under these circumstances? Kendall would never know. She refused to let that sadness stay in her heart for too long. There was plenty of life around her, all worth fighting for. With a baby entering the mix, Kendall knew they had to take Alistair out as soon as possible.

By the time Kendall made her way to her car, she was thoroughly distracted with all the new possibilities. Fingering the ultrasound copy, she tossed her things in the car and felt something slip over her mouth. A nasty aroma filtered through her nostrils, and she felt the world go dizzy around her. Kendall tried to claw at the hands that were now dragging her across the parking lot. Her last thought was to scream for Kam.

Kam! Help me!

Terror gripped her as the world went black. All she could think about was the life that was barely a glimmer in her future.

CHAPTER 20

Kam heard Kendall's screaming plea echo inside his mind. His heart sank as he realized he should not have left her alone today, but she had wanted to run an errand on her own. He had learned from his brothers' mistakes. He had to let her do some things on her own, or she would push back against him when he really needed her to listen.

So far, they had not been able to locate Alistair, but they had also prevented him from attacking the witch's camp, so they had counted that as a victory. The past few weeks, he had been watching her around the clock, spending as much time as he could with her as they got their house together. When he wasn't there, someone else was with her. He had been lucky that Kendall had not seemed to mind the company. Today, though, she had seemed a little worried, as if her mind was preoccupied with something else entirely.

Kam slammed his fist into the nearest tree and jerked it back in reflex. "Damn it."

"Something wrong?" Kyle had just come up behind him.

"Yes. He has Kendall." Kam nursed his wound and saw the bright red blood starting to pool where he had ripped his skin. He deserved every ounce of the pain that came with the throbbing appendage.

Kyle reached into his back pocket and pulled out a bandana he often carried with him when he was landscaping. "What? How is that possible? Didn't she have someone with her today?"

"No, damn it. She wanted to run an errand, and I let her."

Kam was now filled with self-disgust. If anything happened to her, he would never forgive himself. She was his life. He should never have let her go off on her own. At the same time, he could not keep her locked away forever. He had known as soon as she tired of painting and decorating the house, she would turn back to her quest to find Alistair. Had she gone looking for him today? Was that what her errand was about? Why would she keep that from him?

Because he would not have let her. He let out a disgusted breath. If he had just listened to her and let her track him, maybe this would never have happened. Even so, she had been adamant about waiting for the super moon when the witches' powers would be the strongest. He had thought he had some time to prepare for this, but apparently, he had no control over the situation. Kam didn't like feeling helpless.

"We'll find her. Can you sense her?" Kyle attempted to redirect him.

"No!" And that made him even more furious with himself. Her words haunted him. What if he never saw her again? Never held her close to his heart? He squeezed his eyes shut and put his hands at his temples as a loud roar left his mouth. "I'll kill him!"

Kyle held his hand up. "Relax, Kam. It's going to be all right."

"Easy for you to say, you don't have a mate!"

It wasn't like Kyle had any idea of the fear of losing a mate. She was his other half. His life was not complete without her. If she was lost forever, he would walk into eternity alone. His wolf growled inside him, ready to shift into a frenzied fever and take anything and everyone out of his way.

"Wow, just hit me where it hurts." Kyle shook his head at him. "I'd kill to have a woman like Kendall. I'd kill to help you keep her."

"I know." Kam's voice was soft and tortured. "What am I going to do if I can't sense her?"

"We call on someone else to help us, right?" Kyle nodded back to the inn.

"The women?" Kam was slightly dubious. How were they going to help? He was the most direct line to Kendall. If he couldn't feel her, no one else could, right?

"You do realize witches are amazing trackers, right?" Kyle reminded him. "And we have some of the most talented witches on the face of this earth right there in that house."

Kam didn't wait for him to say anything else. He ran as fast as his legs could carry him. When he shoved the door open, his voice was loud and hurried. "Mother!"

Amber Knight came out of the kitchen. "Kam, you'll wake the...what's wrong?"

"He has her."

He felt his eyes watering uncontrollably as anger and fear made him imagine the worst. Kam no longer had a handle over any of his emotions.

"Who has her?" Brina asked from the dining room.

"Alistair. That asshat has Kendall, I know it."

191

Kam ran a hand through his hair and fought the rage that threatened to take over him. His nails ripped against his head, stinging his flesh along the way. The burning pain was a distraction from the fear that was racing through him.

"How do you know for sure?" asked Lila from the stairs.

"She called for me. And then...." His mind was haunted by his next words. "Then she went dark."

"Dark?" Amber's face was now filled with deep concern.

"I can't find her. It's like he cut off my radar. That only happens if...." Kam did not want to consider the end of that thought. If this was it...he just couldn't let himself go there.

"Not always," his mother reassured him. "Sometimes, it happens when your mate is unconscious. Come, ladies. Let's put our heads together."

"What can we do?" Kyle had just come in behind him.

"Keep your brother calm." Amber waited for Kyle to understand her words.

"On it." Kyle put a hand on Kam's shoulder.

"Fuck off!"

Kam jerked his shoulder away from him. He didn't want reassurances. They meant nothing right now.

"Sit your ass down!" Kyle shouted at him, so loud, the room shook. Everyone in the room turned to look at him.

"Fuck wad," Kam grumbled as he sat down on the sofa. Since when had the little twerp gotten a spine? He snarled at him when Kyle sat down next to him.

"Takes one to know one," Kyle returned as he rolled his eyes.

Kam knew his brother was just trying to help him, but Kam couldn't help it. Kiego was ready to rip someone to shreds, and if his brother wasn't lucky, he would take the brunt of his attack. That was just the truth of the matter.

He closed his eyes and tried to find her with his mind's eye, but he barely got a read on her. He breathed a sigh of relief. That meant she was still alive. For how long, he couldn't be sure. The idea that she would be lost forever entered his thoughts, and he shook in fear. Kam had never been afraid of anything in his life. Not like this. Even dodging bullets targeted at his head had not made him feel this way. Maybe that was because it wasn't his life he was worried about. It was hers. He did not want to live in a world where she did not exist. That world was flawed and broken. He had lived that life for far too long.

Opening his eyes, he watched the three women pull together in a circle. Their hands held onto each other as they used their magic to cleanse the room. When they had created a powerful space, Amber pulled out a map of their area, and Brina pulled a crystal pendant out of her pocket. He marveled at their ingenuity as the three of them sat around the map. Two of them held their hands over it, and a bright white light filtered through their fingertips.

Brina closed her eyes. "I call upon every guide, any light that can lead us to our sister in need."

Brina held the pendant over the map, and it started to circle around the map. Kam watched it move in fast circles as the magic tried to locate Kendall. It started to slow, and then, as if pulled by a magnet, it made a small circle, and the chain was pulled toward one spot.

Brina pulled the pendant up and looked at the map. "The old tire factory."

Kam tried to jump up from the couch. Kyle held him down. "Wait, Kam. We need to have a plan."

"I've got a plan. Rip his ass to shreds." Kam growled, and his eyes flashed dangerously. He didn't need any other plan.

"Yes, but we're going to need their help. Remember, this isn't just about Kendall. There are other lives in the balance too. That's why they need to help us." Kyle nodded to the women who were now standing strong together.

"What about...?"

"Kenton Knight! Get your ass down here," Amber yelled upstairs.

A shuffle of steps came on demand. "We're having a tea party."

"Good. You're on kid duty."

"Wait, what?" He looked down at her like she had lost her mind.

"Alistair has Kendall," Kam tried to explain.

"Then why am I staying here?" Kenton pushed his sleeves back like he was ready to dig in and take action.

"Because this is a woman's work." Amber's chin rose in the air as if she was waiting for him to challenge her.

"Very well. Off you go." Kenton had already learned not to mess with his wife when she flashed her eyes at him. "I'll keep these little ones in check."

"I'll pray for you," Brina grinned at him.

"Lovely," Kenton muttered before he raced back upstairs to watch the five children who were probably already destroying the room upstairs.

Kam was prepared to shift into his wolf, but he knew that taking the van would be much faster. He took the keys off the wall and nodded for them to follow him. "Get what you need. We leave in five minutes."

Kam waited outside for the others to join him, trying to calm the wild beast inside him. Kendall had made a good argument for preserving the life of the dark caster who had been enslaving innocent witches and turning them into shades of their former selves. He wasn't sure he could stick to his promise at all. Not when her life might hang in the balance. To hell with the consequences. He would protect her life at all costs. That was the way he was wired. There was no other choice for him.

"Relax, Kam. We'll save her." Karter's voice popped up beside him.

"Where the hell did you come from?"

"You didn't think Lila would not tell me, did you? Let's kick the shit out of him." Karter ground his fist into his hand.

"At least you understand." Kam nodded to Kyle. "That one thinks I should calm down."

"Calm isn't a word in your vocabulary right now. I feel you, man." Karter put a hand on his arm. "We're going to get her."

"Yes, we are." Killian had just pulled his car into the drive. "I'll take the freeloaders, you take the women."

"Agreed."

Kam unlocked the doors and slid behind the wheel. If they didn't get out here soon, he was going to take off without them. At that moment, the women came out, each one carrying a bag filled with various odds and ends. He acknowledged them gruffly when they entered the van.

Turning to look at his mother, he saw her reassuring

smile. She nodded to the wheel. "Let's get this show on the road."

That was all he needed. Kam put the van into drive and pulled out of the parking lot like a bat out of hell. He was not about to waste any more time.

CHAPTER 21

When Kendall awoke, she had no idea how much time had passed. Enough for Alistair to bring her to his new dungeon, apparently. She found herself chained to the wall, and tried to pull her hands out of the cuffs. Not again, damn it!

Kendall slammed her fist into the ground. She heard the shuffling of movement not far from her and heard his voice call out to her.

"So you got knocked up again, did you?" Alistair moved close enough for her to see him holding the ultrasound picture of her baby.

Kendall glared at him. She was not going to give in too easily. If he thought he was going to hurt her again, he had another thing coming. "Go to hell, Alistair."

"You first, Kendall." His hand snaked out and wound into her blonde hair. He yanked her head backward and whispered in her ear. "I think I'll let you think about just how I took care of the last one."

Kendall fought the wave of revulsion that wracked her body. "Fuck you."

He slapped her face with his hand and licked the blood from her lip off his hand. "Still tastes good. Can't wait for more. Looks like I'll be feasting on embryo tonight."

Kendall spit in his face, and almost fell back against the weight of the fist he slammed into her face. Standing on her feet, she was seething with anger. If she had the chance right now, she'd rip his throat out herself.

"Ta-ta, for now, sweet Kendall. I'll be back as soon as I get all my supplies."

Kendall seethed as he disappeared from sight. A fire burned bright inside her. Every inch of her wanted to protect the child inside. The more anger she felt, the more her energy vibrated inside her until something unexpected happened. Her hands started to change before her. The large fingers retracted, and white fur started to sprout from the pores of her skin. The arms turned to legs that slid through the cuffs as if it were second nature.

Sharp claws dug into the ground as she snarled into the darkness. Kendall wasn't sure what kind of magic possessed her right now, but she would definitely use it to her advantage. Her new wolf form delved into the shadows where Alistair would not expect her. When he looked around for her, then she would make her attack. She could escape, but the only way to make sure he never bothered her again was to end this here and now.

In the corner, she waited with a fierce need to kill programmed into her skin. Fight or flight didn't exist. Now it was fight or die. She would not be the one dying today, and neither would her child. Not if she had anything to say about it. Her senses were ignited. His smell wafted near her, and she knew he was coming back. She waited there in the shadows he had once forced her to walk within, and this time she used them to her advantage.

With enhanced eyesight, she saw Alistair creeping toward the chains where she had been just moments before. He saw she had broken free from them and cursed. "Damn it. Where are you?"

As soon as he turned around, Kendall leapt at his throat. He never saw her coming. She felt the crunch of bones under her teeth as she ripped into his throat. He tried bringing his athame up to strike her, but she snapped her teeth closer together, breaking his neck before he could move. Kendall growled as she ripped into his skin. Swiping her claws at his face, she obliterated every inch of his face, erasing his picture from her mind.

She heard footsteps coming down the stairs and turned, snarling at the invaders.

"What the hell?" Kyle held his hand up. "Um...Kam?"

Kam pushed him out of the way and held his hand up. "Whoa...calm down."

Kendall was so far into her rage that she barely registered any of their words. She snarled at him and gnashed her teeth together.

"What do you want us to do?" Amber asked him.

"Take care of the women. I've got this."

"What do you mean?" Killian asked him. "Why don't you just take that one down?"

"I plan on marrying her, you jackass." Kam shook his head at his brother.

"Holy fuck." Karter shook his head. "How in the hell...?"

"I'm not entirely sure, but if you don't go now, she's going to lose it completely." Kam pushed them behind him.

"Get out now."

Kendall paced the room, her paws now covered in blood. The frenzy that had taken over her was hard to push through.

"Kendall…." Kam lowered his body to the ground and held his hand up. "It's okay, love."

Kendall snorted angrily and leapt onto Alistair. She stood on him like the king of the mountain as she snarled at Kam.

"I know. The first is always the hardest." Kam sighed softly and sat down on the ground.

Kendall sniffed the air and felt something familiar breaking through. An earthy smell that had been so calming just that morning. She sat back on her haunches and watched him warily.

"That's it, Kendall. You can push through it." Kam held his hand up to her, and she snapped at it with her teeth. He barely escaped her reach.

Kendall saw the pain in his eyes, and something clicked over in her brain. She backed up a few steps and tilted her head at him. She whined slightly when a tear fell from his face.

"Come back to me, Kendall." He held his hand out to her again.

Kendall's ears fell back, and she paced back and forth a few more steps before a slow huff of air left her mouth. Creeping forward slowly, Kendall sniffed his hand. Closing her eyes, she saw every memory of him swirling inside her brain. A loud howl left her mouth as she started to change back to her human self.

"Kendall!" Kam caught her before she fell to the ground.

She flung her hands around his neck and held on for dear

life as she realized what had just happened. Her entire body started to shake as the adrenaline left her body. Before she knew it, a loud wailing filled the basement. It took her a few moments to realize that it was her.

"Shhh…it's all right, love. I've got you. He can't hurt you ever again." Kam held her tightly against him and stroked her hair lovingly.

Kendall pulled away and put a hand to her mouth. She felt the blood that surrounded her face, and her stomach revolted. Turning away from him, she lost everything she'd eaten that day. A hand flew to her stomach and tears fell down her face. If anything had happened to the baby, she would never forgive herself.

"Are you hurt? Let me look at you."

Kam's hands roamed over her face, and she winced when he found the cuts near her lips and the bruise that was now forming near her eye.

"I'll kill him."

"I think I already did," she whispered in response.

Kam chuckled. "That you did."

"I'm sorry, Kam."

She hadn't planned on killing him, but now she understood why he had wanted to. The fierce protective nature that raced through their bodies was hard to deny. She was still trying to figure out how she had transformed. Kendall looked at her hands and blinked in confusion.

"You have nothing to be sorry for, love."

Kendall felt her anger rising as she thought of what he had planned to do. She stood up and walked over to his body and started to kick him with every inch of her force. She felt

Kam's arms pulling her away from him, but she fought him. Breaking free from his hold, she looked in Alistair's pocket and found the one thing that meant the most to her. Holding the picture in her hands, she turned to Kam with tears in her eyes.

"What is it, Kendall? What did he do to you?" Worry filled his eyes when she reached for her stomach.

"Can we get out of here?" Kendall had a lot to tell him, but this was not the time or the place.

"Yes…but you are going to tell me, Kendall."

She nodded as the tears fell from her face. "Who's going to take care of this?"

"The boys will. Out you go."

As they made their way up the stairs, Kendall started to feel light headed. The last bit of energy faded from her as Kam caught her in his arms. She laid her forehead on his shoulders. "Sorry."

"Don't mention it," he whispered as he nuzzled his head against hers. He carried her up the stairs with very little effort.

When her eyes met the bright glare of the afternoon sun, Kendall realized she hadn't been down there for long at all. Shielding her eyes, she tried to get down, but Kam refused to let her. "I think I can walk now."

"Too bad," he cut her off with a gruff voice. He opened the back door of the van and sat her down inside it. "Now, let me take a look at you."

His hands roamed over every inch of her face, then down her arms, looking for any injuries. When he found her hands folded around the piece of paper, he looked up at her. "What is that?"

Kendall blinked and looked down. Then she realized that she was the only one that knew. Tears fell down her face. "I have to explain. You're going to want to sit down, Kam."

"I'm fine, Kendall, just—"

"Sit your ass down, Kameron Knight." She felt her eyes flash hot.

"Wow…those are damn unnerving," he grumbled as he sat down next to her.

"Now you know how I feel," she snorted.

"So…?"

"When Alistair had me trapped long ago, he took complete advantage of me, without precautions. When he found out I was pregnant…."

"What happened, Kendall?"

"He…." She gulped. "Took care of it himself, which is what caused all my internal scarring."

"I'll fucking kill him."

"Kam…remember…he's dead."

"I could still dismember the asshole," he snarled.

Kendall let that thought mull in her head for a second, and almost considered helping him, but she held her hand up. "Listen, Kam. I told you that we might not be able to have children."

"Yes. And that's not an issue, Kendall. All I need is you. I told you that." He put a hand on her cheek and stroked it lovingly.

"What if there's more?" she asked him.

"I don't understand." He looked perplexed.

She handed him the paper and let him take a look at it. "I was having some pain and had not started my cycle. With my mother's history, I was worried that I had…."

"Cancer?" His eyes were troubled. "Is this a tumor?"

"No. That is our child." Kendall pointed to the small jelly bean in the picture. "Right there…see this? That's the heartbeat. Strong."

Kam's mouth dropped open. "Are you saying what I think you're saying?"

"You're going to be a father. I'm going to be a…." Kendall couldn't finish her words because tears started to fall down her face.

Kam pulled her into his arms and stroked her back. "Shhh…love. It's going to be all right."

"What if I lose it?" She sobbed against him.

"I'll take extra good care of you, Kendall. I promise."

She sniffed slightly. "I hope I didn't hurt the baby. I have no idea how I transformed like that. Has that happened to any of the other mates?"

"Not in our clan, but it does happen in rare instances."

"I'm still trying to figure out what happened to the scarring." She put a hand to her stomach. "It was there. I know it was."

"Ah…I think I know the answer to that." He grinned at her confused look. "We tend to be extremely fertile, and we often have the ability to heal our mates."

She put her hand on his face and smiled softly. "Your love made me whole again."

"I was never complete without you, Kendall."

A voice cleared behind them. "If you're done with the love fest, I've got a report."

"Kyle," growled Kam, who turned around and saw the

sadness on his brother's face. "What's wrong?"

"We were only able to save two of them. We were too late for the others. According to one of the women, he was planning on killing all of them. Even...."

Kendall felt Kam tense beneath her and put a soothing hand on his arm. "Kam...relax. I need you to stay calm for me."

"Calm for...." He looked down at her stomach and cursed softly. "I'm calm, I'm calm."

"Good boy. Can we go soon? I'd really like to wash this off of me." Kendall gestured to the blood that was staining her clothing.

"Yes. Tell Killian I'm taking his car."

"No prob." Kyle looked over Kendall. "You all right?"

"I suppose."

"Good, cause that was fucking wicked," Kyle said with a grin.

Kendall pursed her lips and shook her head. "Hopeless."

"Always," teased Kyle.

Kam picked up her hand and kissed it softly. "Let's go home, love."

"Yes. Home."

Kendall was already picking colors for the nursery in the back of her mind. She refused to think of any other future than the one where she could hold his child in her arms.

CHAPTER 22- EPILOGUE

Kam paced back and forth in the hallway. The midwife had refused to let him stay in the room with Kendall. Apparently, any time she howled in pain, his wolf threatened to break loose. He didn't like seeing her in pain at all.

"Everything okay, Kam?" Killian asked him.

Kam looked at his brother, who was the picture of calm. "How is it I'm the only one that got kicked out of a delivery room?"

"Because the rest of us know how to keep our beasts under control." A loud scream echoed from the room before them, and Killian had to hold him back. "Relax, Kam. That's normal."

"Normal? That sounds like bloody murder to me." He ran a hand through his hair nervously. When he removed his hands, he saw a few strands had come loose. "If she keeps this up, I'm going to go bald."

Killian chuckled. "It won't stop there."

"How did you get through this?"

"The truth?" Killian asked him.

"Yes."

"Mother gave me some herbs to keep me calm." He

grinned at him.

"Where's mine?"

"Hey, you were mister fix it. Everyone expected you to be calm and collected."

"I hope she forgives me." His words were hollow even to his own ears.

"Trust me, after she squeezes that kid out, she'll think of nothing but the baby in her arms. Do you have your names picked out?"

"Yes. But we're not telling anyone yet."

"Still don't see why you wanted to wait to find out what you were having. Mother almost shit a brick when you did that. Especially when you refused to let her figure it out herself."

"That needle and pencil is just an old wife's tale." Kam shook his head.

"If that were the case, you would have let her do it," Killian taunted him.

At that moment, the door slid open, and Amber Knight came out with a huge smile on her face. "It's a—"

"Wait!" Karter rushed over. "We're not all here yet."

"Son of a bitch, Karter. Let her speak." Kam was beside himself with nervous energy.

"Hey, just because you didn't get in on the pool doesn't mean the rest of us aren't invested," Karter grumbled.

"I'm going to kill him," Kam threatened.

"Gee, it's not even me this time." Kyle's smile was obnoxious.

"I'll add you to the list."

Kam walked over to the door and pushed inside, no

longer waiting for anyone to give him permission. He saw Kendall kissing the top of a small baby with a tuft of red hair.

"She looks just like you," she beamed up at him. "She's perfect in every way."

At that moment, he heard Kyle hoot loudly outside.

"I take it they all thought it was a boy?" He asked her.

"He had ten to one odds." Kendall smiled. "Do you want to hold her?"

The ghosts that had plagued their lives were distant memories now. They had not had another death in the hollows since Alistair had left this world. Kendall had not shifted into a wolf either. That could still happen, especially if anyone ever threatened their child. That he was sure of.

"Can I?" His voice was filled with emotions he could never translate.

"Of course. Besides, they have to stitch me up a little." Kendall grimaced slightly.

"What do you mean?" Kam asked as he scooped the infant into his arms.

"She's going to be as big as you, I think. She's already off to a whopper of a start. Ten pounds eleven ounces."

"Wow, she's a toddler," chuckled Kam.

Kendall giggled and winced. "Ouch."

"Are you all right?" He was filled with instant concern.

"I'm wonderful. Now, take Arabella out to meet her family while they finish this, please."

Kam nuzzled his daughter's nose with his own. "Arabella Lucy Knight, you are going to knock them dead one day, my little warrior princess."

About the Author

Ever since childhood, Elissa Daye has enjoyed reading stories as an escape from life. When she was a teenager, she started to write her own stories that kept her entertained when she ran out of books to read. When she was accepted into Illinois Summer School for the Arts in her Junior year of High School, she knew she wanted to become a writer. Elissa graduated from Illinois State University in December 1999 with a Bachelor of Science in Elementary Education and began her teaching career, hoping to find moments to write in her free time.

After seven years of teaching, Elissa decided to focus on her writing and made the decision to put her teaching years behind her so that she could create the stories she had always dreamed of. She is now happily married and a stay at home mom, who writes in every spare moment she can find, doing her best to master the art of multitasking to get everything accomplished.